Chesapeake Crimes
THIS JOB IS MURDER

IN THE SAME SERIES

Chesapeake Crimes
THIS JOB IS MURDER
**Edited by Donna Andrews,
Barb Goffman, and Marcia Talley**

Foreword by Elaine Viets

WILDSIDE PRESS

THIS JOB IS MURDER

Editorial Panel:
Ellen Crosby, Sandra Parshall, and Daniel Stashower.

This edition is published in 2012 by Wildside Press, LLC.
www.wildsidebooks.com

Contents

FOREWORD
by Elaine Viets

Ever feel like killing your boss?

Me, too.

I write the Dead-End Job mysteries, and I know working for a living is murder. Fortunately, I can take out my job-related frustrations by killing people—on paper. I never counted how many I've murdered in my eleven-book crime spree, but most had it coming.

Fiction is my refuge when a job is bleak. And it's not just my superior who gives me the urge to kill. My fingers have itched to strangle a co-worker. I've wanted to leap across the counter to clock a customer. I've murdered maddening colleagues, executed overbearing executives, and annihilated annoying customers in my mind. There's no blood on my hands. No jail time, either. But lots of job satisfaction.

If you've had those same feelings, I promise you'll enjoy *This Job Is Murder*, the latest collection of short stories in the *Chesapeake Crimes* series.

The other Chesapeake Chapter Sisters in Crime anthologies have launched careers and showcased award-winning crime fiction writers. I'm predicting the fifth addition in the series will continue that literary tradition.

I like this anthology. I've read every story in *This Job Is Murder*, and there isn't a dud in the bunch. How do you like your murder: Hard-boiled? Warm and cozy? Fast and funny? Dark and brooding? You'll find it here. My Chesapeake Chapter brothers and sisters in crime have worked wonders with your favorite mystery subgenres.

David Autry turns in a fast-paced thriller with "Deadrise." Harriette Sackler delivers a historical tale of revenge with a twist. "Mean Girls," Donna Andrews's take on office politics, makes you feel the helpless rage of a hardworking woman forced to work with bootlickers. Cathy Wiley's meeting planner discovers a body that was definitely not on the agenda in "Miked for Murder."

Bosses, good and bad, abound. Ever worked for someone who acted as if he was God? Then you'll appreciate Barb Goffman's tale of a man on a heavenly mission. Karen Cantwell doles out the death penalty to a spouse-stealing boss.

In *This Job Is Murder*, even ivory towers are not safe from mayhem. Fans of academic mysteries will enjoy a double dose: "To Adjuncts Everywhere" by Ellen Herbert and Smita Harish Jain's "An Education in Murder."

E. B. Davis takes a shot at delivering justice to husbands addicted to the wild life.

And those dream jobs? Some of them turn out to be nightmares. If you have any doubts, read "Keep It Simple" by Shari Randall and "When Duty Calls" by Art Taylor. C. Ellett Logan writes about the chef who cooks up creepy critters. Jill Breslau tells us about a mediator in a lose-lose situation. And Leone Ciporin gives us "A Grain of Truth."

Working for a living is murder. So is losing your job. Some experts say when a company sacks lots of staff, the survivors aren't lucky. They'll have to do the work of their fired colleagues with less money and fewer resources. They'll work twice as hard to keep those coveted jobs. Their golden handcuffs will turn to lead. And soon they'll feel the urge to kill. The same way you do.

But you need to relax after a hard day. Fix your favorite drink and curl up with this killer collection of short stories. Let *This Job Is Murder* work for you.

Elaine Viets writes two national bestselling mystery series. Her critically acclaimed Dead-End Job series is a satiric look at a serious subject—the minimum-wage world. Her Fort Lauderdale character, Helen Hawthorne, works a different low-paying job each book. *Final Sail*, her eleventh Dead-End Job mystery, is set aboard a luxury yacht where Helen Hawthorne works as a stewardess. It debuts in May 2012 as a hardcover and an ebook. Elaine's second series features St. Louis mystery shopper Josie Marcus. *Death on a Platter* is the seventh novel. Elaine hosts a weekly half-hour talk show, the "Dead-End Jobs Show," interviewing people about the extraordinary secrets of ordinary jobs, on Radio Ear Network (radioearnetwork.com). She has won the Agatha, Anthony, and Lefty awards.

KEEP IT SIMPLE
by Shari Randall

"Well, happy birthday to me," Serena muttered as she pulled into the parking lot of the Dutch Maid Motor Inn. It was her thirty-fifth birthday, but given her current surroundings, it wasn't going to be her best one.

She cut the headlights and drove slowly to the rear of the shabby, one-story building. In a few months the lot would be jammed with the minivans and compact cars of budget travelers eager to hit nearby Mistucket Beach. But it was off season now, and just a smattering of old sedans and pickup trucks sat in the near-empty lot. *Oh yeah, you blend,* she thought, staring at the special edition Jag she'd followed into the lot. It stood out from these sullen old cars like a Vegas show-girl at a church picnic.

Serena chewed her bottom lip and scanned the building. A few moments later light outlined a flimsy curtain in a ground-floor unit. She sighed and reached for a cigarette. A decrepit Volvo and a slow-moving police cruiser had gotten between her and the Jag. She'd seen her targets pull into the motel but missed them walking from the car into the building. She'd have to see what opportunities the window offered.

Serena climbed out of her BMW, pulled a black canvas bag from the back seat, and cautiously circled the Jag. She scurried behind a Dumpster, crouched, and deftly assembled her equipment by the erratic light of the neighboring restaurant, its Waffles 24 Hours sign winking like a lecherous old man.

The curtains to room 112 jerked open. Serena froze. Just twenty feet and a sheet of dirty floor-to-ceiling glass separated her from her targets. Jeez, they must get a thrill out of doing it with the curtains open, Serena thought. Well, it makes the job a piece of cake.

Cheesecake, she amended, expertly focusing a tiny video camera on the zaftig blonde in the motel room.

Serena panned the interior of room 112. "Yup, I'm the Cecil B. DeMille of adultery," she muttered around a smoldering Marlboro, capturing head shots as she had been taught. Establishing identity was the most important thing, her boss, Morty Acerman, said; *otherwise it could be any two (or three or four) wandering spouses in there, see?* And you need to get the Act Itself, also known as Zero Deniability in Morty-speak.

In the year she had worked for Morty, Serena had learned that it was the details rather than the Act Itself that steamed the spouses who hired Acerman Security to follow their wandering mates. When the husband dropped big money on jewelry and trips and flowers for the Other Woman, that's what got them mad. Morty said that he hadn't met the wife in this case but figured she had money; she had sent a hefty retainer through an intermediary.

Serena considered enlivening things with a shot of the voluptuous moon wrapped in a gauzy stole of clouds (traditional romantic imagery juxtaposed with the tawdry reality of the squat cinderblock love nest—once a film major, always a film major), but she came to her senses. Morty had warned her more than once about getting artsy. Keep it simple was Morty's mantra. She appreciated that he left out the "stupid" for her. At least lighting wouldn't be a problem. Every lamp in the room was burning; even the television was on. You guys are making this too easy, Serena thought. Amateurs.

They were both pretty new to the adultery thing, in her opinion. Serena had followed Krystle, a thirtyish elementary school guidance counselor, and Artie, the sixtyish president of Millard Department Stores, from Krystle's townhouse to the Camelot Steak House, the neighboring town's swankiest restaurant and club (if you liked large slabs of red meat and highballs with your senior discount), and finally to the Dutch Maid. They had both worn sunglasses, but Artie left the car's top down. They had been pretty easy to keep in view, especially since Artie observed speed limits and Serena had a lead foot. Even Serena had to admit that tailing wasn't her strong suit. She had been practically on their bumper the whole time, until the Volvo and police cruiser cut her off.

The bed was against the motel room's right wall. Artie and Krystle perched on it like two kids waiting to see the principal. Behind them was a closet, its door ajar. Serena could see that Artie had taken the time to hang up his expensive gray suit jacket, shirt, and slacks. Krystle's silky blue dress hung next to Artie's jacket. Serena noted Artie's shoes and Krystle's blue pumps lined up next to each other in front of the bed. She hummed "Devil with a Blue Dress" while dragging on her Marlboro.

Krystle stood up abruptly and starting shimmying with Artie's tie, then flung it away. She was in pretty good shape, kind of jiggly through the bust and hips, but not bad, Serena thought. Krystle quickly shed a polyester, industrial-strength bra and lace g-string. "Red and black! Tacky, tacky," Serena scolded. She zoomed in on Artie's face. Even through the telephoto lens, the sweat crowning his balding head and the purple flush of his complexion were evident. Hope he lives long enough to enjoy this, Serena thought. *Jeez, if a guy ever looked that miserable about doing a mattress mambo with me, I'd hang up my thong.*

Serena spat out the cigarette, ground it with the toe of her black, high-top sneaker, and returned her attention to the scene on camera. Krystle pushed Artie back on the bed, then coyly pulled up a sheet. Serena yawned. Evidently, Krystle felt that the best way to finish a disagreeable task was to get it over with quickly. Artie's head was wedged between two pillows and was hard to see. After awhile, they both sat back against the tattered vinyl headboard, sheet tucked in under their chins, and shared a cigarette. It was the most intimate and loving gesture of the evening.

Serena glanced at her watch, mentally begging the hands to move faster. 10:30 p.m. Morty had told her to get as much as she could, so Serena leaned against the Dumpster, camcorder at the ready, although she had a feeling she'd seen all the action, such as it was, that would be happening in room 112.

She tried to get the motel room television in the shot, hoping the lovers were tuned in to *Operating Theater.* Monday night stakeouts made her miss her favorite television show. Serena carefully scanned the rutted parking lot. Artie's Jag gleamed like a dull gold wedding band in the darkness. She scrambled to it, careful not to step into the pool of light from the lovers' window, and draped herself comfortably on the hood of the car. She focused on the television screen and paused. CNN? Stock quotes? Weird and kinky.

Serena resumed filming the couple on the bed. Artie had poured himself a generous splash of... She zoomed in on the bottle of Chivas on the bedside table. Krystle sipped from a can of Diet Coke. Only the best for Krystle.

Serena yawned again and stretched as Artie worked on the Chivas and Krystle channel surfed. More than once Serena's head nodded to the cool metal hood of the Jag. She hadn't expected the sheer monotony of the private detective-in-training's life. Following people and filming their most intimate moments had seemed an exciting way to make a living, but after only a few months, Serena had been amazed at how dull watching other people have sex could be.

The late spring air was warm and soft; the murmur of the ocean, only two blocks away, an irresistible lullaby. Serena carefully placed the camera on a mini pod, slid off the car, ran in place, and did jumping jacks. Feeling minimally refreshed, she resumed her place on the hood of the Jag and played Six Degrees of Kevin Bacon. Herbert Lom was in *The Ladykillers* with Sir Alec Guinness...hmm...who was in *Star Wars* with Harrison Ford, who was in *The Fugitive* with Tommy Lee Jones, who was in *Men in Black* with *Will Smith*, who was in *Independence Day* with Bill Paxton, who was in *Apollo 13* with Kevin Bacon! Too easy. Esther Williams—

Movement from the room snapped her back to alertness. Artie was stumbling from the bed to the bathroom. Not surprising after all that booze. Krystle sat at the edge of the bed, glanced at her watch, then rose and yanked the curtain closed. Shadows spattered the flimsy gray fabric as lights in the room were turned off.

"Hallelujah," Serena whispered. The camcorder's date/time icon read one a.m. She broke down her equipment and stowed it in the duffel.

Serena started up her BMW and drove slowly from the parking lot. Once out of the lot, she flicked on the headlights and floored it. The Dutch Maid receded in the rear-view mirror as she sped past darkened T-shirt and souvenir shops and into the drive through of the twenty-four-hour Crusty's Crab Shack. She hadn't eaten anything except some breath mints since she began tailing Krystle and Artie. She shouted her order into Crusty's shell-shaped mike, then picked up a Double Dynamite burger and—since it was her birthday—a large chocolate milkshake from a glassy-eyed teenager at the window. She needed a pick-me-up. Krystle and Artie's encounter at the Dutch Maid was the most depressing assignment of her short career.

* * * *

It was almost noon when Serena parked in front of Acerman Security. The company shared a graffiti-tattooed brick storefront with AAA Pest Control and New U! Weight Loss Clinic.

"So you decided to come to work today, Mata Hari." Estelle Rein, Morty's secretary, barely glanced away from her computer screen as Serena entered.

"Good morning to you too, Estelle."

Morty poked his head out of his office.

Serena smiled at Morty. "Rhett and Scarlett kept me up." So did the Crusty burger and milkshake, she added silently.

Serena handed Morty the canvas bag. It held the camera equipment plus some stills she had printed.

Although he wore his belt a little too high for her comfort, Serena had to admit that Morty still carried himself with the confidence of someone who had once been a G-man. She liked Morty. He had given her a chance when she really needed one. Though he did a tough job for some pretty crummy people, Morty still hustled. Serena didn't want to hustle herself, but she admired it in Morty. And she liked the way he called her "kid."

"Get in here." Morty waved her into the office. "Hold the calls, Estelle."

Serena could feel Estelle's disapproving eyes follow her as Morty shut the door.

Morty shuffled behind the desk in the cramped office, and then sat down heavily on his squeaky office chair. "Heard the news this morning?"

Serena shook her head.

"I taped it. Watch." Morty pressed a button on the TV remote, then clasped his hands as if in prayer, and leaned his forehead against them. Serena sank onto the brown vinyl couch opposite Morty's desk.

A newswoman spoke urgently as wind whipped her hair about her face. She stood before a huge white clapboard house. The ocean visible behind it was a glossy postcard blue.

"Prominent Wavecrest Hill socialite Beatrice 'Bunny' Millard Stanley was found dead early this morning at Millard Hall, her seaside mansion. When the well-known community leader missed a breakfast meeting where she was scheduled to speak, family members and police were called to the home. Police are investigating the death, and sources confirm that an antique handgun from her family collection was found at her side. An apparent suicide note also was found and made available exclusively to the RIN news team by a source close to the family. The note was addressed to her husband, Millard Department Stores President Arthur Stanley. The note reads, 'I can't go on, Arthur. I can't stand to see you unhappy. Once, the gift of love belonged to you and I. Now, I love you enough to set you free.'"

The reporter looked up from her clipboard. "For news team RIN, this is Becca Morecci."

Serena's eyes met Morty's.

"Yeah, that's right, the wife of the guy you tailed."

Serena groaned.

"This thing feels dirty, well, dirtier than usual." Morty opened the canvas bag. "Let's look at that tape."

The intercom buzzed.

"Yes, Estelle?"

"Mr. Acerman." Estelle spoke loudly, distinctly, and nasally. Serena's eyes met Morty's again. Usually Estelle mumbled. This could only mean two things: trouble, or that a good-looking man was in the waiting room.

"Mr. Acerman," Estelle continued with a wounded, maddening slowness. "Detectives Ritter and Falcone from the Oceanview Police Department are here to see you about a matter which they won't discuss with me."

Morty zipped the bag and handed it back to Serena. He pressed the intercom button. "Very well, Estelle. I'm almost finished here. Why don't you get the two detectives some coffee?"

"Now I know it's dirty," Morty said. "Keep everything with you, get out of town, and turn off your phone. I want to look at everything before the police do. Rendezvous at the Sand Dollar at 1800."

Serena resisted the urge to salute. She shouldered the bag and walked slowly and casually out of Morty's office. She approved of Estelle's taste; one of the detectives was a very good-looking blond (wedding band) and the other was even better looking, with dangerous dark eyes and tousled black curls (no wedding band). Serena smiled slightly at them both and then hustled into the parking lot as Morty invited the detectives into his office. She popped into her car and decided to treat herself to some shopping. No reason a girl couldn't enjoy eluding the police.

That evening, after lobster rolls at the Sand Dollar, Serena and Morty drove to her oceanfront condo.

Serena handed Morty a bottle of beer and booted up her PC. They watched in uncomfortable silence, which amused Serena, since as a former film student she found the technical aspects of filming sexier than she found her subjects, and Morty had probably seen more sex acts than a projectionist in an X-rated movie house. She found his discomfort endearing. Morty studiously kept his eyes on the screen, as if making eye contact would embarrass her.

"I called one of my contacts at the department," he said. "The detectives showed up because an anonymous caller tipped them off that Mrs. Stanley had hired Acerman Security to follow her husband. I told the detectives that you'd be returning from out of town early tomorrow morning and you'd give them everything you had."

Morty sipped. Serena nodded. Krystle shimmied on the screen.

"The Stanleys had only daytime help," Morty continued. "The housekeeper left Mrs. Stanley last night around five. She was eating a left-over seafood casserole since her husband was"—he made air quotes—"'at a meeting.' The housekeeper says that Mrs. Stanley believed in a quiet evening and early bedtime on days before she made her public appearances. She began a tutoring program for inner-city kids and was in demand as a speaker to community groups. The housekeeper knew about the affair. She insists that Mrs. Stanley did not. The housekeeper's the one who leaked the note to the TV station. The autopsy is tonight."

As they watched, Serena pointed out several things that had puzzled her.

"With me, Morty?"

"Yeah, kid, we were set up."

"Nobody's using me as their alibi." Serena shook her head. "I still don't know how they noticed me."

"I should have put Lenny on this one. You're the type a man notices, especially a guy with a wandering eye. And more importantly, definitely the type a jealous woman notices." He sipped his beer. "And you gotta work on your tailing. Remember—"

Serena chanted along with him. "Stay back, relax, keep subject in view. And above all, keep it simple." Serena smiled at him sweetly.

Morty's ears turned pink.

* * * *

Serena struggled out of bed at seven a.m. and blearily opened her closet door. Those detectives were cute. She toyed with the idea of meeting them at the door in her bathrobe. *Down girl!* She sagged against the door jamb. Was it her fault that she hadn't had a date in over a year?

Serena virtuously chose a pair of slim-cut linen slacks and a silk blouse, then showered and dressed. Her years as a model made her movements efficient and quick, and she frowned only slightly at her rear view in the mirror. She took her breakfast (orange juice, multivitamin, cigarette) onto the patio and unfolded the newspaper.

A photo of Bunny, a heavy-set woman with the bull-dog sternness of a maximum-security prison matron, glowered from the front page. The text of the suicide note was included, the exclusive scoop to the TV station notwithstanding. The story offered no new developments, except for the difficulty of locating Mr. Stanley the morning after the death. The paper reported that Mr. Stanley had been "on an overnight business trip." Serena guffawed, then turned to the obituaries. "Beatrice 'Bunny' Millard Stanley...only child of the founder of the Millard Department Stores chain...degree from Wellesley, *cum laude*...president of the Oceanview Library Circle...taught English literature at the Stonehaven School for Girls...started an innovative program to tutor at-risk inner-city students."

Serena lifted her thick raven curls, letting the breeze dry the shower-damp tresses. In her work with Morty she'd seen her fill of older men taking up with young hootchies, tossing the wife on the dust heap of his mid-life crisis.

Serena rose and grasped the balcony railing. "I can't go on Arthur. I can't stand to see you unhappy. Once the gift of love belonged to you and I. Now I love you enough to set you free." She shook her head and laughed. "Puhleeze, Bunny! Talk about B-movie dialogue!"

The breeze lifted the newspaper, and Serena scrambled to gather the wind-borne papers. She flattened them, reread the text of the suicide note, then flipped back to Bunny Stanley's obituary. She slowly refolded the paper. "Bunny, they're not getting away with it," she muttered as the doorbell rang.

* * * *

Serena arrived at work disappointed. Two *female* detectives had picked up everything from Monday night and had questioned her, their disdain for her and her profession barely veiled. Hers was equally strong. She had never seen such badly put together outfits. She had given simple, minimal, entirely truthful answers to their questions. She kept her observations and suspicions to herself.

Serena asked Estelle for the Stanley file, pressed some numbers into her cell phone, then took a meeting with Morty over a box of Dunkin Donuts. When she left, she stopped at Estelle's desk.

"Estelle, I have a favor to ask you."

Estelle's green-shadowed eyes narrowed.

* * * *

"Thanks for squeezing me in today," Serena murmured as the middle-aged beautician deftly painted a coat of passion fruit lacquer on her nails.

"Not at all, hon. We're not too busy this early in the week."

"I have a job interview at Millard Department Store, and I want to look nice," Serena lied.

"Oh, really, dear." Anne Marie Curran, owner of Hair Today and Nails Too!, regarded her with watery blue eyes. "Worked there myself many years ago. In Foundations. My first husband is president of it now. And I just heard on the news that his wife killed herself. What a terrible thing." She shook her head, setting dangle earrings swaying. Her heavily mascaraed eyes grew glossy with tears. "I wonder if I should call Artie?"

"Uh—"

"You're right." Anne Marie shrugged off the thought and briskly resumed her work. "I mean, it's been years. We're in the same town, but might as well be in different countries. Artie moved up in the world pretty quick with his second marriage." She tsk-tsked. "What a thing, what a thing."

"Were you and uh, Artie, married long?"

"No, just a couple of years. Artie, he liked expensive things. And she could give him those things." She looked up briefly and stabbed the air with the orange-tipped brush as she said, "Bunny. That was her nickname. Her real name was Beatrice. Her father owned the department stores. Big girl, pushy if you ask me. God forgive me for speaking ill of the dead."

She paused, cupping her chin in a ring-laden hand. "Don't know what she saw in Artie. Well, he was kind of cuddly and old fashioned. What's that word? Like the knights and ladies? Chiv something."

"Chivalrous?"

"That's it. But I like what I got."

"Your family?" Serena nodded to a dozen framed photos.

"My grandbabies. My husband now, Jimmy, we had five of our own. Artie and I didn't have any. Let's just say that my Jimmy has more energy in the romance department." She winked.

Serena laughed. "I like a little energy in the romance department myself."

"Artie, well, things were fine, but truth be told he was kind of shy"—Anne Marie lowered her voice conspiratorially—"in the romance department, if you get my meaning."

Serena nodded encouragingly.

"I kind of liked that about Artie. He was never pushy or anything." Anne Marie paused wistfully. "Not too adventurous. He even liked the lights off. Didn't undress in the light either. But that Bunny didn't look too spicy herself, so they probably worked out fine."

* * * *

Serena pulled into the visitors' parking lot of Oceanview Elementary School and slipped on sunglasses and a hat. After scanning Estelle's files, she had called the office at Oceanview and asked for an interview with Miss Krystle Kawicki. She explained that she was a student at the university hoping to follow a fellow alumna's footsteps into the guidance-counseling field and had a few questions. Fortuitously, Miss Kawicki had a few free minutes that afternoon.

A secretary directed Serena to the guidance counselor's office. As Serena knocked, a pigtailed girl left while Krystle distractedly filed papers and waved her to a couch lined with worn teddy bears. Serena perched on the edge of the couch as Krystle resumed her seat. THE HUGS START HERE read a wooden sign on Krystle's desk. "So what can I do for you, Miss DeMille?"

Serena took off the glasses and hat. "It's about Artie."

Krystle's face remained frozen in mid-smile, but her eyes went blank and wary. "Artie who?" she asked brightly.

Serena pulled a still photo of Artie and Krystle at the Dutch Maid from her bag. She held it just out of Krystle's reach.

Krystle bolted from her chair and yanked down the venetian blinds on her window to the hallway.

"What are you up to?" she hissed, her back pressed to the window.

Serena returned the photo to her bag, careful to keep her movements slow and smooth. Krystle panted with the tightly coiled energy of a cornered animal. Serena casually crossed her slim, long legs.

"Artie's gonna rat you out," Serena said. She could hear the surging murmur and muffled shouts of students changing classes in the hall outside Krystle's office. "Let's face it. You're getting a little soft. Artie's just using you to get all that wonderful money to himself. Sure he has a great job, but Bunny held the purse strings to the real money. And he's gonna tell the cops that you did it, because…" She watched warily as Krystle picked up an oversized teddy bear, her fingernails digging into its soft, stuffed belly. "Because you're the one who arranged the hit. Not Artie."

Bull's-eye, she thought, watching Krystle's eyes narrow.

Krystle's glossy red lips twisted. "You're lying. Go ahead and show that picture to anybody. Artie loves me. An affair's no big deal."

Serena smiled comfortably. "Artie's not your only problem. The guy you hired is. Not Acerman," she explained quickly. "The hired gun. He's a talker. You'd better take care of him. And in the meantime, you might want to give me some cash to keep quiet about your part in it."

Krystle hurled the bear. "What I'm going to give you is a—"

Both women jumped when a little boy jerked the door open. "Isn't it my Teddy Time, Miss Kawicki?"

"Just sit in the waiting chair, Timmy. I'll be right with you."

Serena was impressed by the cheerfully calm sing-song with which Krystle had addressed the little boy. Krystle was a good actress. Dangerously good.

"Let's not hold up Timmy any longer." Serena grabbed her bag. "I'll see you here next week, Miss Kawicki." Serena smiled slowly. "Thanks for the teddy time."

* * * *

Twenty minutes later, Serena chuckled as she watched Krystle race into the parking lot. Like a kid after an ice cream truck, she thought. Serena sank behind the wheel of Estelle's maroon Yugo as Krystle's Jetta screeched into the traffic on Cliffside Avenue. It hadn't been hard to convince Estelle to switch cars for the day. Morty said never tail the same subject in the same car. Serena let a couple of cars slip between the Yugo and Krystle's Jetta. "Stay back, relax, keep subject in view. And above all, keep it simple," she chanted. Her cell chimed. A text message from Morty: *Founders Park*. Serena smiled; she hadn't known where Krystle would go, but she was pretty sure what she would do.

She followed Krystle to Founders Park and was gratified to note that Krystle had parked her car directly next to Artie's Jag. Krystle scurried down the path to the lakefront. Serena scanned the parking lot. Minivans occupied the slots nearby. A minivan would be great cover, Serena thought. But the guy she was looking for would drive a—*bingo!* Serena pulled Estelle's Yugo next to a hyper-masculine, custom Suburban. It was parked near the exit, out of the mainstream, ready for a hasty exit. Like a pro. She snapped a photo of the license plate and then strolled onto the path Krystle had taken.

"Kid," called a voice from behind a newspaper. Serena joined Morty on a park bench overlooking the lake.

"Well?"

"By the paddle boats."

Morty flipped casually through the sports pages of the *Oceanview Observer* as Serena pretended to snap photos of the ornate Victorian boathouse.

Through her powerful zoom lens, Serena focused on two men leaning on the railing overlooking the boat basin. One was Artie, holding a large, plastic Romantic Antics shopping bag.

"The bag's a nice comic touch." Serena focused on the man to Artie's right. She whistled. "Big biceps."

"Yeah." The *Oceanview Observer* curled down. "The hit man. Name's Donnie Urbanski. Works for State and National Transport. They're a front for the DiNuzzo family. He's Krystle Kawicki's cousin."

Serena watched events unfold through her camera like a silent movie. Urbanski leaned casually on the low railing, watching the paddle boats churn the calm lake waters. Like King Kong in a philosophical moment. Artie inched nervously to Urbanski's side and pressed the bag into his hand. Irritation ruffled Urbanski's bland facade.

A blond blur moved into Serena's view. "Here comes Krystle. I think we're gonna have a Jerry Springer moment."

The *Oceanview Observer* and Morty stood to get a better look.

Krystle strode with tight control toward Artie, then whirled and sucker punched Urbanski. The big man's arms windmilled as he bounced off the railing and staggered to regain his balance. Urbanski rearranged his sunglasses and smoothed his hair, then walked away as unobtrusively as a burly man carrying a lavender shopping bag could. Artie pulled Krystle toward him, stroking her towering blond hair. She slapped away his hand. She was too involved in her tirade to notice that two joggers had stopped Urbanski. Neatly bundled stacks of currency tumbled to the ground as Urbanski dropped the shopping bag and attempted to run, but was efficiently subdued. Two women sitting on a nearby bench then rose and flashed badges at Artie and Krystle. A police van and two cruisers screeched into the parking lot. Serena felt a fleeting stab of sympathy as Artie cringed. Krystle flailed at Artie and then at the women who attempted to peel her off him. Serena wasn't surprised to see Krystle clawing and pulling the undercover policewomen's hair as they struggled to cuff her.

"I knew she'd fight dirty. Time to roll the credits on this little comedy." Serena slipped the camera strap over her shoulder and pointed to a hot dog cart. "Hey, they've got Grote and Weigels."

Morty insisted on paying. "Wasn't it your birthday Monday?" he asked. Serena beamed. They sat at a picnic table by the parking lot, watching along with a crowd of curious mothers, children, and senior citizens as the cruisers and van pulled away.

"So the police were watching Artie anyway." Serena shook a mustard packet and bit it open.

"Yeah. You always think about the spouse first. Glad you got Kawicki here in time to incriminate herself. Urbanski may have given her up, but Artie's definitely the type to try to protect a woman. Even if she doesn't deserve it."

"Chivalrous," Serena said.

"Krystle'd be on the first plane to the Bahamas." Morty chewed appreciatively. "Then when Artie's—well, Bunny's—money ran out, she'd probably find herself another sap. But it all worked out. Just a couple phone calls and presto. Sting operation. Kawicki and Stanley caught red-handed paying off the hit man. Cops more than willing to take the credit." Morty's eyebrows rose. "Speaking of which…"

"Hey, Morty." The two undercover joggers joined them. Falcone and Ritter from the office. They looked even more devastatingly handsome in jogging gear. To her horror, Serena felt a large gob of mustard drip from her hot dog onto her shirt.

"Good to see it worked out." Morty nodded toward two empty spots at the table.

"Thanks, Morty. Serena, right?" Falcone said.

Serena nodded and wiped the mustard furiously. Her mind went momentarily blank as the men settled their sweaty, athletic frames onto the benches.

"Grateful for your help, Morty, but you've got to tell me, how'd you put it together?" Ritter asked.

Morty grinned at Serena. The men turned to Serena, Serena's eyes met Falcone's, and she forgot about the mustard.

"Because we had nothing solid," Ritter continued. "No forensics from the house. Side door left conveniently unlocked, so no break in. Autopsy showed Mrs. Stanley slightly sedated, just enough to make it easy for a hit man and not enough to seem suspicious."

"Easy enough for hubby to put something in her dinner before he left for the night." Morty nodded. "Could even be seen as part of the suicide attempt."

Serena tore her gaze away. "I can see Artie doing something non-confrontational and sneaky like that, especially if under orders from Krystle."

"Miss Kawicki." Ritter frowned. "My kids go to Oceanview."

"Kawicki's Donnie Urbanski's cousin," Morty added.

"Nice family," Serena and Falcone said at the same time.

"Owe me a coke." Serena smiled at Falcone. His ears turned pink. Morty cleared his throat.

"The big problem was your surveillance," Falcone said. "Talk about a rock-solid alibi for Kawicki and Stanley. The medical examiner put the time of death between seven and midnight."

"And I tailed them from six until one in the morning. Alibis Are Us." Serena sipped a Pepsi thoughtfully. "Still, seems like a pretty embarrassing plan for him. I mean, he's off with his girlfriend while his wife's committing suicide."

"Yeah, but what an alibi. Not only witnessed, but recorded," Morty said.

"What made you think it wasn't suicide?" Falcone's deep brown eyes turned shrewd.

Serena took the last bite of her hot dog, and chewed slowly, savoring.

"It was the shoes and the 'you and I'," she said.

Ritter looked blank. "The shoes and the you and me?"

"Exactly. At the Dutch Maid, their shoes were lined up together, just like little soldiers. Their clothes were hung up. Let's just say that keeping the room tidy is not the first thing two people in a motel room have on their minds. Plus the curtains were open—on the first floor—and every light was on." She licked mustard and relish from her fingers. "They made it too easy."

"They could have been, what, exhibitionists." Morty dabbed his lips with a napkin.

Serena nodded. "That's the first thing you think of. Remember the first job you sent me on, with the retired trapeze artist and the state senator?"

"Heh, heh, heh." Morty chuckled.

Falcone's eyebrows shot up. Ritter laughed.

"But I talked to the first Mrs. Artie. She said he liked the lights off. Sure lots of guys change with a new woman, but then there was the 'you and I' from a former English teacher."

"I don't understand," Falcone said.

Morty grinned.

"The suicide note said, 'Once the gift of love belonged to you and I.' Bunny was an English teacher. She never would have written 'the gift of love belonged to you and I.' It should have read, 'the gift of love belonged to you and me.' When I heard it on TV, I figured it was the reporter making a mistake. Then I read the text of the suicide note in the paper. The pronoun should have been in the objective case."

Morty raised his can of soda in tribute. "Smart girl."

"So you two cooked up this sting based on some shoes and two little words." Falcone smiled.

"Freakin' awesome," Ritter said. His cell buzzed. Ritter glanced at the screen. "We gotta go."

"Morty." The detectives shook hands with Morty, then Serena, with Falcone's hand lingering a second too long.

"Serena, I'll have to give you a rain check on that coke." Falcone grinned and walked up the path.

Morty and Serena tossed their trash. "You know, Morty, they didn't even need that flowery suicide note. They should have kept it simple."

"There isn't too much simpler than greed, kid."

Serena watched the detectives. Falcone threw not one but two glances back her way.

Or men, she thought.

Shari Randall works in children's services in a public library. She lives in Virginia with a wonderful husband and has occasional visits from two globe-trotting children. She enjoys dance from ballet to ballroom, antiques, and mystery fiction.

ALLIGATOR IS FOR SHOES
by C. Ellett Logan

People'll knock off anything. That's what I was thinking as I waited on the porch of the big, obviously faux country house, not in a rural area at all, but behind tall brick fencing and ferocious iron gates in a suburb of Atlanta. Before I could bang the bronze armadillo-shaped knocker, a rangy man with skin as wrinkled as alligator hide appeared in shorts that seemed to billow without a breeze, black socks, and those rubber shoes they stick you in at the spa.

"Um...I'm Nonni Pennington?" Not used to sounding professional, since this was my first job (unless you count marrying up), the end of my statement came out like a question—an affectation I thought I'd shed after high school ten years ago. I cleared my throat and continued, "Mr. Shelbee is expecting me." Mr. Shelbee was Chef Clyde, the Citchen Critter's star, who'd become famous cooking unusual dishes featuring game or farmed exotic animals.

"That's right," the man said and turned back inside. I followed.

After a few paces in his wake I yelped, "What *is* that?"

"*That* would be simmering fish heads," he replied. "For stock."

I wasn't talking about the smell, only, God knows, it was awful. Frozen in mid-flight on top of an armoire in the foyer loomed a stuffed bird with its splayed talons pointing at my head.

My guide, unmoved, continued across the dining room as I scurried to keep up.

A voice from the next room called out, "Emmett, why are you hollering?"

The back of Emmett's bony hand stopped me beneath the archway to the kitchen, its frame gleaming with intricate wood carvings of fruit and fowl.

"Chef, that P.I. my daughter hired for us is here," Emmett said. "Should we come in?"

We must have gotten the nod, because in tandem we entered the kitchen. I noticed a red brick floor and a cozy fire in an eye-level hearth directly across the room, right below a stuffed 'possum on a shelf, its tail artfully draped.

An elfish man wearing bike shorts and no shirt stood on a stool in front of the longest counter I'd ever seen. The chef was done up in an apron that only partially covered his bare chest. The Citchen Critter logo was printed across its bib.

"I'm put out that Ms. Turnbow is not here in person," the chef said to the ceiling as if in prayer for divine patience. Then he turned to me. "My culinary assistant, Pilar Heinz, is missing." He punctuated each syllable by stabbing the air with a fat knife. "Less than one week before the Gastronomic Gambles championship. I need you to find her. Now!"

"My employer has sent me to do the initial interview," I stammered, "since, as she informed you, she's at a sensitive point in another investigation. If we get the basic details of your case to her right away, we can begin the background checks." I liked the term background checks. Sounded so detective-speak.

Loris Turnbow, my aunt, had been kind enough to give me a job with her P.I. firm after my husband embezzled his company's largest fund, then fled the country. She served as my training officer, helping me meet the minimum requirements set by the state board to get my license. It was no secret that she hoped I'd make this temporary solution to my cash-flow problems permanent. She apparently thought I had promise.

"Doesn't she look like Pilar?" the chef asked as Emmett handed me a photo of the missing person.

"I declare, she does."

"Ask your questions, girl," the chef commanded.

Even though he had to stand on a stool to be eye-level with me, I fought the urge to run. To cover my nervousness, I dug in my Fendi bag for paper and a pen to take notes.

I dropped that pen when I noticed a dozen bird feet, toes up, on the countertop in front of Chef Clyde. The medieval-looking contraption hanging over us, where pots and unfamiliar implements of all shapes and sizes dangled, didn't help.

Thankfully, a sign above the stove, "No Road Kill Used in the Preparation of This Dish!" made me laugh and regain my composure. I picked up my pen and forged ahead with my questions, determined to do the job right.

Before I'd left the office, my aunt had explained that this was a bad time for her to take a new case because of an issue with an employee. Since only her son and I worked for the agency, I took that to mean my cousin had stepped in it. Again. That left me. She explained that Emmett's daughter, a client several years ago, had called in a favor. Sending me to do the light lifting would jump-start Chef Grumpy's case.

Emmett ferried a covered dish from the refrigerator to the counter. "I have a plan, Chef, to find Pilar. Young lady," he said turning my way. "I think my idea will assist you as well."

"What idea?" My aunt hadn't said anything about the clients having ideas involving me.

"It will be far more difficult to find our culinary assistant than you imagine," Emmett said. "Winning the Gastronomic Gambles is *all* to some people. They've worked hard for many years to get to the final round. Any attempt to snoop will cause suspicion. They'll assume you're trying to sabotage them, even if you explain you're only trying to find Pilar."

"People take this stuff that seriously?"

"She's so naïve," the chef said and climbed down from his stool. "No one will talk to a detective, or any outsider, during the run-up to the taping. I doubt you'll even be allowed on the set."

"Why not let the police handle the investigation, then?"

"The police," Chef Clyde said, a sneer on his pointy face, "did a cursory investigation and found nothing irregular. Pilar isn't a minor. Adults can disappear if they want to."

"Back to my idea," Emmett said. "Ms. Pennington here can pose as our new culinary assistant."

"What?" The chef and I said at the same time.

"Think about it, Chef. I'll assist you, like in the old days, and she can assist me. That will provide the perfect cover. She'll be assistant to the assistant, so no one will pay any attention to her. She'll find out things we'd never be privy to."

"What about the release for Pilar's recip—"

Indicating the kitchen with a Vanna White sweep of his hand, Emmett silenced the chef mid-sentence. "We'll practice preparing the menu here," he said to me and gave his final pitch, "I have an old co-worker at the studio who will get you set up."

"I hope you know what we're doing," the chef said, sing-song, and turned back to his critters. He was through with me.

"The only thing that matters," Emmett said as he walked me to the door, "is that we get Pilar home safely."

I agreed to the scheme. I wanted to solve this case to show my appreciation to my aunt for offering me a job and for opening her home to me. I might be sleeping on a divan on her sun porch, its sheets falling way short of the thousand thread count I'd grown accustomed to during my high-end marriage, but on the bright side, I was getting exfoliation treatments for free.

* * * *

I was feeling a little cocky as I sped down the sidewalk. I'd survived my first interview on my first assignment. Then the heel of my shoe caught in a crack in the flagstone walk just outside the iron gate. As I bent over to ease the heel out of the hole without marring the delicate alligator leather, a man walking toward me from the yard next door called, "There you are. Thought you done run away." The snowman-shaped gardener reached me. "Oh. Sorry. Took you for Pilar. Same color hair."

My shoe popped free.

"So, I take it you haven't seen Pilar recently," I said brushing crumbled mortar off the hem of my pant leg.

The man continued to look me over, all five feet of me, plus my three-inch cheat heels and said, "If I was her, I'd stay gone."

Trying to follow my aunt's instructions not to discuss a client's case while being nosy and chatting people up at the same time (*wha?*), I tried my hand at questioning the witness.

"Why do you say that?"

"'Cause everyone knows she's the real artist in that kitchen. Chef Creepy Critter makes use of her recipes and talent, then he takes all the credit."

I was out of questions. This looked so easy on TV. Luckily for me, it appeared the guy took my hesitation as skepticism and added, "You think I'm full of it? I wasn't always wider than I am tall. Pilar brought me her practice dishes, sometimes two or three a day." He kissed the fingertips of one hand.

"If what you say is true, why would Pilar work for a man like Shelbee?"

"She gets to develop her dishes, and when the time is right, make her move to get her own show." He headed back toward the neighboring yard, then turned. "I don't know how she does it. I got ambitions. But I ain't got the patience to put up with an asshole like Shelbee. Maybe she just reached her limit. Hope not, though. Sure would miss being her guinea pig."

* * * *

When I got back to the office, I explained the plan. After my aunt finished laughing, she struggled to put away her snarky face and put on a mentoring one.

"Whew. Sorry. The picture of you in the kitchen even pretending to cook was too much."

"Your approach to confidence building could use some work," I said.

She shrugged. "So if you go in as the replacement assistant, we could get onto the set before the rehearsal and filming?"

"That's right. Evidently, there's always camera crew, company reps, and assistants running around the set. Since I'd be the new girl, it'd be only natural for me to have questions. And I'll have two days after rehearsals to see what we can uncover before the actual taping."

"You'll need to bone up on the production of a cooking show and the duties of a culinary assistant, or you'll never pass as someone hired for competition. Ask Emmett to email the dishes, recipes, and ingredients they've planned. Study those." She got her cell phone out of her pants pocket.

"You've seen me try to boil water. This is going to be a disaster," I moaned. "All of TV land is going to see me crash and burn."

"Man up, girl." She thumbed her phone. "I just emailed a couple of websites to you."

There was her famous empathy again. "Can't I just do the paperwork that's piled up around here? Until I've gotten a few easier jobs under my belt?" I'd be real good at billing. I handled my own credit card accounts when I was married.

"You need to learn the business. How to work undercover. Plus, being out there will give you the client contact you need."

"But I don't like clients—or even people, for that matter."

"Exactly. On that note, someone claiming she'd been Pilar's culinary school roommate called. Said she'd heard that Chef Clyde hired us, and she wants to help. I didn't confirm that we have the case, but check her out—see what her angle is. Perfect opportunity to get real-world experience. Here's the address."

I researched the Gastronomic Gambles competition and checked all the social media for something on the roommate. The cooking show even had its own Facebook page, but I found no e-presence for the roomie whatsoever. Looked like Auntie would get her way and I'd have to actually make *contact* with the staff at the cooking school as part of the roomie's background check.

When I checked my email, Emmett had already sent the requested information. The dishes:

First Course—*Cajun Turtle Stew*
Second Course—*Fig-Glazed 'Possum Kabob on a bed of Quinoa*
Main course—*Squirrel Ravioli and Truffles on a bed of Poke Salad*
with a side dish of
Asparagus Wrapped in Poached Alligator Tail

God. A person should get a warning before opening a message like that. At the very least, there should be some kind of gross-out filter that captured unsavory email until you can face it.

Holding my breath, I sat down to read the rest of the nightmare that was to be my life for the foreseeable future. When I got to the phrase "mince the squirrel meat," I closed my eyes and let the held-breath out slowly. Eventually, the universe stabilized enough for me to continue reading the distasteful document, even though I skimmed it like gravy.

At "scald, dress, and pick the hair off the 'possum," however, I headed to the bathroom, hanging my head over the toilet bowl until the wave of nausea passed. The office toilet—which the public used. Where does one go to recover from that?

Gumshoes grumbling their way across television and movie screens suddenly made sense. The monosyllabic responses of down-and-out private eyes, the drinking, the bitterness. Call me a house dick, I'd be surly too. Knock me in the head with a gun butt, and I'd be cranky. Already, getting people to tell me things they never meant to tell anyone, snooping into matters that weren't any of my business, and pretending to be someone I'm not had frayed my last nerve.

* * * *

I'd never been on this side of town, with its boxy little houses, all the same, all in a row, and it took getting lost twice to find the address. The driveway ended in a ratty hedge instead of a garage. Behind the glass of the front door, a dark-haired woman nearly filled the frame, and didn't speak until I was on the porch right in front of her.

"You must be Ms. Pennington from the Turnbow Agency." She moved aside and opened the door to let me in. "I'm Denise Quay." We sat down on a settee in the foyer.

"You called our agency to voice a concern about—"

"The disappearance of Pilar Heinz. My friend did not just wander off, no matter what the police say." She sounded angry instead of concerned.

"You mentioned to Ms. Turnbow that a Gastronomic Gambles chef might be involved."

"Clyde Shelbee. He's gotten away with so many things in the past, why not murder this time?" The woman was wringing her hands as if a neck was between them.

"Murder is a very serious accusation," I said as softly as I could so I didn't rile her any further.

"If you'd had dealings with the famous Chef Clyde in the past… Pilar finally saw him for the jealous and petty little man he is. She wanted something in writing this time guaranteeing she'd get credit for her contributions."

"If he refused, maybe Pilar finally said enough is enough and took off."

"No. Pilar might quit, but not until after the competition. She believed if she could get Shelbee to acknowledge that the recipes were hers, it would launch her career."

"It's my understanding that Chef Clyde is going ahead with using Pilar's dishes in the competition."

"What? And the network is going to let that bastard get away with it?"

"With what? If you have evidence that a crime has been committed, you need to go to the police."

She stood abruptly and marched to the door. "You have more than enough evidence already to get the police to swear out a warrant on Shelbee. Instead, you're going to allow a killer to cover his tracks." She shoved the door open with her foot. I guessed our chat was at an end. Seemed my detecting skills were shaping up nicely.

* * * *

I called my aunt's cell to report what little I'd learned.

"Where are you right now, Auntie?"

"Angelina hired us to tail Brad," she replied. "I'm at the Four Seasons having a mojito, waiting for him to come out of the bathroom with the barmaid."

"Ha ha. Do you want to hear what I learned from Pilar's friend?"

She sighed. "Not now. I'm still dealing with the case your cousin screwed up. The client wants that boy's head on a plate."

"I thought it was just a misunderstanding."

"My son's description of the problem as a *misunderstanding* was a bit of an understatement. I'd give you other choice words, but not over the phone. At any rate, you'll have to keep handling the Heinz case."

"Handling? As in making decisions?"

"Don't panic."

"Don't panic? It's a little too late for that!"

"Listen, I love you and want to be supportive. I just can't deal with your drama right now. Come back to the office and type up your report."

"I was going back to your house to soak my feet. They're killing me."

"Well, maybe tomorrow you'll wear sensible shoes."

* * * *

When I returned to the office, I found a woman with ash blond hair, clad in a tan running outfit sitting alone at my desk. She clutched a huge khaki purse.

I asked the beige lady, "Does Ms. Turnbow know you're here?" My aunt didn't want me to call her *aunt* in front of clients. Said it wasn't professional.

"Are you Nonni?"

"Yes. Do I know you?" I sat on the edge of my desk and looked down at her.

"No, but you've met my father. Emmett."

"And?"

"He and I haven't seen eye to eye these last few years. Not since he decided to keep working for that tiny tyrant, Chef Clyde. But he's still my father. If something has happened to Pilar, my father might be in danger, too."

"Are you suggesting that Pilar's been hurt, or worse? And your dad might be next?"

"It's common knowledge that Clyde sabotaged competitors in the past in order to win cooking competitions. Who's to say he didn't take his shady behavior to the next level?"

Emmett's daughter was looking down at her cradled purse. When she raised her eyes to meet mine, they were glossy with tears. "Pilar would not leave before showcasing her family recipes on national TV. It doesn't make sense. Why not wait until after the Gastro Gambles to leave?"

She smothered her face in a wad of tissue and came up blowing her nose, then disappeared into my aunt's office.

This P.I. stuff sure involved a lot of emotional roller coasting. Thank goodness Emmett's daughter had brought her own tissue because I wasn't equipped to offer my shoulder to every weepy person I encountered. Wasn't too many weeks ago I was on my own amusement park ride to hell.

* * * *

The Gamble's studio was in a section of mid-town Atlanta lousy with warehouses and wholesale storefronts. At the end of a string of concrete-block clones, it stood out as the only two-story structure in the queue.

The lobby's appointments were spare and its glass abundant. The security officer looked like security officers everywhere. I had to sign in and show ID, then I was instructed to wait. After a few minutes, a girl in her late teens bopped up to me with her hand out, blue nails sparkling, to shake mine.

"Are you Nonni Pennington?"

"Yes."

"I'm the production assistant. Come on down to the Green Room, and I'll get the staffer handling support cast to go over the waivers with you."

With that, she nearly skipped out of the room. I followed, trying to avoid the cables snaking this way and that, and to process what I was seeing as we sped through the hallways. Open crawl spaces and exposed duct work made the place look more like an electronics warehouse than the prestigious venue of a renowned cooking competition.

The Green Room was pale peach. A woman at a desk, hunched over a laptop, turned to us with an annoyed look that she didn't bother to wipe off, even after Skippy the P.A. introduced me.

The sourpuss staffer's name was Mare. "I'll get you a copy of the script and some releases you need to sign," she said. "Emmett emailed me that he'll be the primary assistant and you'll be the second. Hope you can take pressure." She and the young girl walked off discussing the problem of teams poaching one another's shelf space in the refrigerators.

Emmett had called to say he was on his way over to drop off overly large ingredients needing refrigeration, after which he wanted to show me around the studio kitchen. I needed to at least *look* competent. Later, we'd go do a dry run of the actual dishes back in Chef Clyde's kitchen to ensure the recipes remained secret.

I plopped down at the desk in the peachy Green Room, thinking for a second of tossing the drawers. Before I could act, Mare walked back into the room, handed me the documents, and turned to leave.

"Wait," I said. "I was hoping you'd answer a couple of questions."

"Why would I help you help Clyde? He never did anything for me but put me down, work me to death, and take all the glory for himself. Seems that's a habit of his, so watch out."

"Nobody told me you used to work with Chef Clyde."

"*Used* to, and I'd cover the show of every prima donna chef on this network before I'd work one more minute for Shelbee."

"Look, I'm just trying to do a good job."

She crossed her arms over her chest and leaned her hip against the door jamb. "Hell, you seem like a nice person, but you are one soufflé away from a collapse if you don't get out now. I'm deadly serious. Ask yourself why Pilar would disappear just days before a contest she worked her ass off to win."

Less than a minute later, Emmett came through the Green Room door, brushing right past Mare. At the sight of him she began to sidle out of the room.

He saw her out of the corner of his eye. "Mare! Thanks for getting Nonni the releases."

"I don't understand how you can still work with him, Em. And drag this gal into it." Mare was scowling and shaking her head.

Emmet set his packages on the counter. "We owe it to Pilar."

"Don't hand me this 'we' crap. How sick is it if she's not here to enjoy the triumph won with her dishes?"

"We don't know for sure that she won't turn up before taping."

Mare held up her hand. "I don't have time to go into this with you right now." She looked at me and said, "Good luck. You're gonna need it." Then she was gone.

"If everyone thinks I'm incapable of handling this," I said as huffily as I felt, "why keep me on?"

"We all want to find Pilar. I'm too visible, too suspect, to be of real use. We need you to poke around and uncover the truth."

In the back of my mind, I wondered if suspect might be the perfect word for Emmett. It had been his idea to step in as first assistant. How'd he put it? "Like back in the old days." Did he maybe think he wasn't visible *enough*?

* * * *

A couple hours later I had my first lesson in the chef's kitchen: how to scrub my hands until they were raw and cram all my hair up under a hideous cap. The trouble began when they tried to teach me the difference between a utensil and a serving piece. If only the contest could be about the variable microwave warming times of say, frozen entrees versus leftover lo mein...

"I've already removed the entrails, glands, the head, and the tail." Chef Clyde's face was as red as the carcass on the counter. "I don't understand why you won't look at the 'possum. How do you expect to pass yourself off as my assistant if you won't even look at it?"

Pissed, the chef charged out of the room. Emmett gave me a look of sympathy and then followed.

With my lessons apparently over, I wandered over to some nearby shelves with cookbooks, awards, and framed photographs, including several pictures of Pilar and of Pilar's culinary school roommate. Denise wore a chef's hat and was holding up a trophy, posing with Chef Clyde in what looked like a studio kitchen. Why hadn't she mentioned she did the same job as Pilar? Was being an insider the reason she *knew* the chef was guilty?

* * * *

The next morning, I went to the studio early, hoping to get comfortable enough with the set that I wouldn't screw up later during rehearsal. I approached the door to the dark lobby of the studio. The security guard and his desk, however, were lit like the display window of an anchor store at the mall. He kept his head down even as I popped off my last acrylic nail jerking on the door handle. I rapped on the glass with my car keys, and he let me in.

"The morning crew hasn't come in yet," he said as he returned to his seat and the electronic game he obviously found so enthralling. "They usually don't turn on the lights until seven."

"That's okay," I said, "I just wanted to get more familiar with the equipment before..."

I shut up and headed to the set because he was intent on the game again. I took this opportunity to slide into a couple of storerooms along the way, as well as some offices, but I didn't turn up any clues to help me find Pilar. I hoped I'd find something on the set.

The only light on the kitchen's set was the wavy red glow of the exit signs and the LEDs of the electronics equipment. When Emmett had shown me around the day before, the lights had been blinding, coming at me from every direction, and they were hot, too. I preferred this low-watt mode, and only switched on a light above a sink.

Separate areas of the kitchen had been assigned to each team. I went to stand at our deep stainless-steel counter with its sink, stove, cutting board, and so many sharp knives it looked like we were filming an Xtreme Autopsy show. Right behind me were the refrigerators. I had a cheat sheet with the locations of our ingredients in the open cupboards under the counter. I did a quick inspection then came back to turn the stove's burners on and off, try the faucets, and practice controlling the high-powered hose attachment that could fill a large pot with water fast.

Every sound I made seemed unnatural, echoing down low at first, then rising to be abruptly absorbed and dampened by the high ceilings, really rattling my nerves. It was dawning on me that the closer we got to taping without Pilar showing up, the more likely it was that I'd have to take the stage, risking exposure.

Opening refrigerators required bracing myself. I couldn't actually see Chip and Dale and Bambi inside the transparent containers, only imagined I did. Thankfully, Emmett had tasked me with prepping the produce and gophering things around, excuse the pun, giving me the perfect opportunity to question the film crew, all innocent-like. And if we actually had to take the plan down to the wire, Emmett would be the one to brave the critter carnage and the chef's temper.

Nearby, in the off-set darkness, something crashed to the floor with a metallic clang.

"Emmett?" I called. Nothing. I looked down the hall, but I didn't see anyone. "Hello? Does someone need to use the kitchen set?" I thought I saw a figure moving along the corridor leading to the lobby. I grabbed my purse and tried to catch up.

As I approached the front, I heard Emmett chuckle and the guard say, "Hey, I'm almost outta here. Don't be asking me for nothin'."

I stepped into the now fully lit space. "Emmett, did someone come from the direction of the set just now?"

"No. Why?" Emmett crossed the lobby and peered down the hall.

"I came in early to go over the layout one more time, and I thought someone—"

"You'll be fine," Emmett interrupted, then greeted a man and woman entering the lobby.

The three headed down the hall, turning on lights as they went. I followed, feeling anything but fine.

* * * *

Thirty minutes later, the studio was filled with busy culinary assistants, make-up people, and camera crew. Booms were raised overhead. I watched as a hand-held camera operator near our station, seemingly sporting a camera where her head should have been, paced off the space. After a while we were told to stand down while the show's production crew went through their checklists.

I hadn't thought to bring breakfast and was starving, but not for some little forest-creature omelet. I knew better than to look for something normal in the refrigerators near the set, so I went to a break room offstage I'd noticed earlier. The room was empty and dark, but I didn't turn on the lights—didn't want to advertise to the staff that I was pilfering food. The hall was short enough to spill light in from the set anyway. Monitors, keyboards, old phones, and broken chairs filled the corners, but there were no desks to rifle. I could just make out motor sounds—the fridge was on. Maybe I'd luck out and find string cheese or some yogurt that wouldn't be missed.

I pulled open the door. It wasn't a large refrigerator, but then it didn't need to be because Pilar was so petite.

I didn't shut the door as I backed away and plowed into a pile of cast-off small appliances, sending it flying. Good thing. The racket silenced the entire studio for the split second it took me to get out a high-pitched wail. I added, "Help," as I stumbled into the hall and slid down the wall outside the break room, my eyes bulging and glued to its doorway. From my seated position, I watched people move past me as if in slow motion. Their screams were strangely muffled.

Someone was at my elbow, urging me to stand. "Come on, Nonni, let's get you away from here," Mare said. She walked me to the far corner of the set. Skippy had produced a chair from somewhere, and they eased me onto it.

"Put your head between your knees if you feel faint, honey," Mare said.

"Uh, uh."

"Shhh." Mare tilted my head back and looked deep into my eyes. "You're going to be okay. The police are on their way." Then she and Skippy went to join the murmuring knot of people in shock outside the break room.

I continued to process things in slow motion: Chef Clyde looking lost at the very back of the crowd, Emmett at the front, while our hand-held camera operator filmed everything. The camera was trained on Chef Clyde, but I didn't think the chef noticed.

"Everyone move back," Emmett said as he gently pushed people. "The emergency crew will need to get a stretcher in there. The police will not take kindly to the way we're trampling the crime scene." Chef Clyde had already moved all the way over to where I sat.

The camera operator continued to aim the lens at the chef, even though it required jockeying for position in order to shoot around the people filing back into the kitchen. I was about to say that something didn't seem right about this, when someone in the lobby screamed, "Dead? Pilar's dead?" startling everyone.

The hand-held operator jerked her camera to the side for a fraction of a second.

"Denise is a camera operator, too?" I inquired of no one in particular.

But Chef Clyde heard me and backed up against the storage racks, shouting, "That's not a cam—that's Denise. Emmett! Who let *her* in here?"

Denise threw the camera down, and the room full of people gasped as one. She was moving toward the set side of the counter. I followed her gaze, realizing she was heading straight for the arsenal of knives. When I saw that Emmett was trying to head her off, but wouldn't make it, I jumped out of my chair, grabbed the hot water faucet handle, and turned it for all I was worth. As soon as Denise got to the opposite side of the counter from me and put her hand on a knife handle, I aimed the hose and spewed the steaming water right into her ear. She screamed and flailed and crawled into a cupboard under the counter to escape. My hand was frozen. I couldn't let go of the nozzle until a police officer came up beside me and turned off the spigot. I stared, hypnotized, as water continued to flow and drip from surfaces high and low. I kept staring, craning my head over my shoulder, as I was led away.

＊ ＊ ＊ ＊

Much of what happened after that was a blur. Best forgotten anyway. I heard that the Gastronomic Gambles folks delayed the filming of the competition indefinitely out of respect for Pilar.

At Pilar's memorial, Chef Clyde took responsibly for her death, explaining that Denise had apparently committed the murder to make him suffer. When killing Pilar didn't derail his quest for the trophy, Denise planned to end him with his own deboning knife during the competition. Knowing his murder would be taped was the icing on the cake.

"Actions have consequences," Chef Clyde said. "Six years ago, Denise Quay was a talented chef, and I was a judge for a major competition she'd probably have won. I disqualified her without grounds, and everyone went along with my decision. I was jealous, vain, and vindictive, and as a result, a very dear friend has paid the ultimate price. Please forgive me."

I never learned of a single person who did, but I'm sure the little chef felt better after baring his soul. I'm also sure network executives felt better after removing the chef and his show from their lineup.

Emmett retired to work in his herb gardens full time. Denise's scalded face healed, and she's hoping to avoid prison by claiming temporary insanity.

I learned many things in my first job—like solving a culinary case is tougher when murder's on the menu. And I learned it's not always true that crime doesn't pay. My aunt split the fee with me. I'm on the way to Tootsie's Boutique with my half to see if they sell sneakers in alligator.

C. Ellett Logan spent the first half of her life in the Deep South, an experience that informs her settings, and troubles her characters, southern-Gothic-style. Now in Northern Virginia, she's a member of the Chesapeake Chapter of Sisters in Crime and Mystery Writers of America. Her stories "Backseat," "Anchors Away," and "Alligator is for Shoes" show off in the *Chesapeake Crimes* anthology series (Wildside Press). Her novel, *Miasma*, part of the Quagmire Murder Mysteries, is set in Georgia's low country. www.celogan.com

NEXT STOP, FOGGY BOTTOM
by Karen Cantwell

Athena Papas didn't fall off the platform onto the tracks the way they reported it on the news. She was pushed.

How do I know?

Because I pushed her.

Then I watched happily as the screaming train crushed her thin, limp body like an empty aluminum can. It was a good day. And while she probably would not agree, I would say it was a good death. Not many people hated Athena as much as I did. Trust me, I had good reason, and not just because she'd been my boss. It was so much more. Every day during the ride from New Carrolton to Foggy Bottom, I listened to her blathering into her cell phone while she flipped through another edition of *Washington Bride Magazine*.

"We're meeting with another caterer tomorrow," she said one day. "The last company was a disaster. They were inexperienced and unorganized and kept trying to push the chicken on us." She flipped another page and shook her head. "No. I don't want chicken. Too common." The pages kept turning and her glossy, painted lips flapped on. "And they don't even do the cake. I want someone who does it all. Is that too much to ask?"

Blah, blah, blah. She made me sick with her crimson fingernails and milky skin. Her black hair as soft and shimmery as the surface of a calm lake on a summer's day. Her pencil-thin waist and perfectly small, pretty feet. Sick, sick, sick.

The hum of the train on the rails, the gentle bobs and turns lulled my churning soul. Lights strobed in the tunnels while the PA announced stop after stop. Smithsonian. Federal Triangle. Metro Center. Finally, three stations later, they'd call it, "Next stop, Foggy Bottom."

For other passengers, relief was in store. But not for me. She never stopped talking on that damn phone even as she stepped off the train and walked the four long blocks to the office of Hillard, Smithwick, and Rowe. "Mom," she'd say. "I want you to meet Terry before the wedding. Come for Mother's Day." Then she'd laugh. "Wait until you see the diamond. It's the size of Texas." Her graceful arm would be crooked at the elbow, holding a fancy bag, while the diamond twinkled. Truthfully, she exaggerated. It was more the size of Vermont, but either way, it was big. Bigger than my all of my pathetic chips put together.

Then a full day at the office where she held the title of office manager, but played the part of office beauty queen. She probably would have worn a swimsuit to work if allowed, just to add pizzazz to her already disgusting flirtations. "Oh, Mr. Hillard," she'd coo to the hundred-something founding partner, "if I didn't already have a fiancé…" On a daily basis, my mind simmered, figuring out ways to shut her up.

She would even talk to strangers on the underground platform at Foggy Bottom while waiting for the train home. "My fiancé," she once told some bored lady in a gray suit and tennis shoes, "said I could have the biggest wedding I wanted, so I'm making him keep his promise." Her bleached white teeth gleamed when she smiled, her fancy bag dangling effortlessly from her arm while she tapped a lime green pointy toe. I never could have stayed upright in heels as high as the ones Athena wore. Black flats were more my style.

Once I decided to kill Athena Papas, I had to calculate the most effective method. I wasn't very strong so I never would have been able to strangle her. Not even close. I couldn't shoot a gun. Poisoning was out of the question. My options were limited. After following her for some time, it became obvious that the best plan would be to push her off the platform at Foggy Bottom. The trains there moved fast, the platform was quite high, and the crowds were big enough to make it look like an accident.

My problem was that Athena didn't have a habit of standing particularly close to the edge. She often hung back, chatting with some stranger or on her cell, waiting till the last minute when the train arrived, then relying on her beauty and the kindness of willing men to let her pass through the crowd. Irksome. But I had all the time in the world to be patient. I knew that one day, the time would be right.

As it turned out, I didn't have to wait very long.

She must have been distracted by her own conversation. "But, Terry, sweetie, handsome man that you are," she purred. "You don't understand. I don't care...what? Margaret? I don't care about appearances. I want...hello? I said, I want my wedding my way!" She shook her head and tapped her foot. "Hello? Terry? I can barely hear you." Her shiny tresses bounced around her shoulders like in a shampoo ad. "Terry, we'll talk about this when I get... I don't care about Margaret's family. Who are they to me?"

Luckily, poor Athena was becoming increasingly frustrated. Her voice raised by octaves and decibels. She was inching closer and closer to the edge of that big, beautiful, dangerous platform at Foggy Bottom. I looked at the digital clock. The express train to New Carrollton would pass soon. Because it didn't stop at Foggy Bottom, it would sail right through at breakneck speed. The Fates were on my side. My time would soon come. So would hers.

Athena Papas would pay for what she had done to me.

For stealing my husband.

It happened at that office Christmas party—I know it. With her unblemished skin and her soft hair. Her fancy bags and her perfect teeth. She had everything I didn't, and he fell for it like a fat man on a tightrope. It didn't matter that I loved and adored him. That I slaved for hours every Sunday making his favorite meal of roast lamb with orange marmalade sauce, fresh steamed, French-cut string beans, and mashed red potatoes with a four-layer, double-chocolate cake for dessert. That I washed his underwear, ironed his shirts, and remembered his mother's birthday. None of that mattered to Terry, who I once called husband and now called The Devil. The man she called Sweetie, Handsome Man.

I had practiced the push for weeks, building up the strength and the ability to get it just right. It wasn't easy. There's an immense learning curve to mastering the art of moving mass. Not all of us can do it. I needed the right amount of power to bump her skinny, taut body right over the edge, into the path of an oncoming train.

A heavy hum from the tunnel let me know the train was on its way. Lights on the platform blinked to warn passengers back. Athena was too engrossed in her own world. "Margaret is not my problem, I'm telling you——." Her eyes flashed with anger; her free arm waved about like a marionette limb on strings. "Not my problem!"

She didn't know the train was there. She didn't know I was there.

It wasn't hard to access my own anger—the energy I needed to pull this off. It boiled endlessly within me like a desperate, churning volcano.

With the train in sight, I did the deed. Exactly as I had practiced time after time. One simple bump.

"Next stop, Foggy Bottom!" I shouted the words, rejoicing in the triumph.

Athena toppled, as if in slow motion. Her cell phone sailed high into the air. Her fancy bag fell to the platform, where it teetered helplessly on the edge. Time stood still as the lime green, glittery show of materialism seemed to struggle to hang on—as if it had a life of its own and did not want to die. Eventually the bag lost its fight. It tipped too far and fell onto the rails, just in time for the cars to slice them both like a hot knife through butter. Athena and her fancy bag. Dead. I wondered if the ring survived.

Then came screaming and mayhem. Not one person considered it anything but a tragic and unfortunate accident that this beautiful woman had tripped on her own tall, spiked heels at just the wrong time. No one noticed me at all.

For a moment, I almost felt sorry for her. I knew how it felt after all. To die. To have my life stolen from me when I was still so young. Of course, I was murdered by my own husband who wanted to be rid of me and, more importantly, needed the insurance money to marry his new, popular, prettier love. And since Athena was the reason I was dead, the pity never came.

When the dust settled and passengers were moved from the scene, Athena stood on the platform next to me in her new form. Confused, no cell phone, no fancy bag, she batted her long lashes at me.

"Margaret?" she asked. "I…I don't understand." She scanned the platform, as if looking for answers. A fireman passed right through her. She yelped. Her eyes reflected the fear I remembered so well when I discovered that my body and I were no longer one. When, from across the room, I first viewed my carcass sprawled on the hard tile of my kitchen floor while Terry scurried about, testing different locations on the floor to place the unused EpiPen I'd "dropped." Wiping down the counters then placing one tiny shrimp in my bowl of leftover fried rice from Hunan Feast. I had no one there to greet me as I greeted Athena now.

"Down there," I said, motioning to the bloody scene on the tracks. "That's what you get, Athena Papas." I was so pleased with myself.

"You did that to me?"

I smiled. She wasn't as stupid as I thought. "What do you think, pretty feet? And your Terry, sweetie, handsome man—he's next."

Leaving Athena behind to contemplate her earthly demise, I found my way to Terry. We spirits move effortlessly, once we learn the ropes. Then I waited. I wanted to be there when the police rang the doorbell to notify Terry about this oh-so-tragic accident.

Later, at the kitchen table that was once mine, he sobbed uncontrollably. The tears he'd cried for me were only for show. When family and friends left the room, his eyes had dried faster than desert sand. It felt good to watch him suffer for real.

Fully intending to capitalize on my newfound power, I had planned to continue my reign of revenge, exacting a similar fate on the man whose bed I once shared, whose love I practically begged for. The man I despised even more than the wretched Athena Papas. But as I observed his obvious despair, it occurred to me that death would be too good for him. They would only end up in each other's arms again.

No, I decided. Death would not suffice.

His suffering must be greater. Longer. Enduring.

And so it is.

Athena has found us, but she's weak. All she does is moan.

Not me. I'm hard at work every day seeing to it that Terry the Murderer, Terry the Devil, Terry, Sweetie Handsome Man understands the true meaning of torment.

And when his doctors and family and psychiatrists don't believe him when he tells them of the strange events that befall him—doors opening and slamming of their own accord, mugs shattering in his hands, knives flying through the air, narrowly escaping his throat, the endless wailing—I just laugh.

And the best part?

I know he hears me.

Karen Cantwell has been writing plays and short stories for many years. Her short story "The Recollections of Rosabelle Raines" was published in *Chesapeake Crimes: They Had It Comin'*. She is also the author of the funny bone-tickling Barbara Marr murder mysteries, *Take the Monkeys and Run* and *Citizen Insane*. These days, if she's not kicking back, watching movies with her kids, Karen can be found at her laptop, conjuring a third Barbara Marr novel, *Silenced by the Yams*.

LUCKY IN DEATH

by E. B. Davis

"Mrs. Decker, you don't have any sales experience." The large, bald man looked up from my job application and leaned back in his desk chair.

Baldy had eaten too many grits and enjoyed a few too many libations around the campfire. I'd known a few like him so he didn't faze me. Besides, after yet another dog-panting August day of trying to convince someone to hire me despite my age, I was desperate. ProTrout was the last place I wanted to work. But I was experienced in hiding the truth so Baldy would never know.

"Bet I know ProTrout's inventory better than most of your sales help," I replied.

"Really. How come?"

Probably not a good idea to tell him what ProTrout had done to my marriage.

"My husband drooled over every item in this store. In fact, my garage is filled with so many fishing lures, rods, reels, tackle, and accessories, I still can't get my car inside."

"A die-hard customer, I presume."

"You can say that again. Joe died a year ago."

"Wait...Decker. Are you Joe Decker's widow?"

I nodded.

"What a shame. I couldn't believe after years of wanting a fishing boat, he up and died after he finally bought one."

"He didn't just buy a boat," I said. "He bought the whole damned package—outboard motor, GPS, fish finder, even a trailer and a boat cover. All paid for in cash. Forty thousand dollars." Every penny I'd saved for my granddaughters' college fund. But Baldy wouldn't care about that any more than my no-good, long-gone son-in-law did.

"I remember," he said. "Nice man. I'm so sorry." He stared at the floor while he talked, subdued, almost contrite.

"Thank you," I said. "He dropped dead the day after he bought it. And you wouldn't take the merchandise back."

"No, once the boat was in the water and the engine immersed, I couldn't take it back as new. Company policy, I'm sure you understand." Baldy looked at his shoes like a little boy confessing to soaping the neighbor's windows. No, I hadn't understood.

"I sold it on eBay," I said. "Only got twelve thousand dollars."

"I'm glad you got something from the deal."

"Enough to pay for his funeral."

"Joe sure was a great fisherman," Baldy said. He looked uncomfortable, making me glad, but then his discomfort wouldn't get me the job. And I needed the job to rebuild that college fund.

"I may not have sales experience," I said. "But I know the merchandise, what it's used for and how to use it. I accompanied my husband to every stream, river, gulf, and backwater around here. Who do you think baited all of those hooks?"

"Sounds like maybe you could sell, but most of our customers are men who wouldn't take your advice about our gear."

"I can soft sell. Offer pointers, pander to them. Let me prove myself."

Baldy's face looked red, and he patted his forehead with a handkerchief. I knew he didn't want to hire me, but I also could see that his forty-thousand-dollar sale at my expense worked on his conscience.

"I guess you know our customer profile," he said, finally. "I'll give you a try. We'll start you off in the ladies outdoor-clothing area. After a few weeks, if you do well, we'll train you for inventory control and on the register. Do you have clothing that fits into our outdoor theme?"

"Of course, although some are stained. Fishing isn't a clean hobby."

"All you'll really need are canvas pants and some attractive boots. We'll supply a shirt with the ProTrout logo."

The thought of wearing that damned leaping fish on my chest made me angry again, but I managed to smile.

"Thank you for giving me the opportunity," I said. "You won't be disappointed."

He barely looked at me, so he probably didn't realize how I was seething at having to take such a low-paid, menial job at my age.

The next day I started work. The store was busiest at night and on weekends when men were off work looking to spend their paychecks, but I started out working days in ladies clothing, the slowest department. I knew women also fished, but they didn't often shop at ProTrout, which reeked of testosterone and pandered to all of those erogenous male ego zones—the slickest reels, the largest boat, the most powerful engine, the most expensive hunting rifles, and all those electronic gadgets like fish finders—taking the sport out of any sport.

After two weeks and register training, I rotated to fishing tackle. It wasn't a hard sales area, and I knew the merchandise. Most of the customers were replacing lost or worn out items in their tackle boxes. The tackle manager must have reported favorably on my performance, because Baldy switched me to the higher-traffic night shift and gave me a twenty-five-cent-an-hour raise. I didn't like the hours, but I found they passed more quickly when the store was busier.

The weeks went by and daylight savings time changed to standard time. I fell into the routine of the store and took my dinner break just after sunset. Since the employee lounge was unappetizing, I ate in, or by, my car and then smoked a cigarette. I'd quit years ago, but the second after Joe died I'd lit up. Stress will kill you, they say. Down to two per day again, I enjoyed my smoke, hidden by the all-terrain vehicles showcased next to the parking lot.

Customer traffic slowed at the beginning of November. Management assured me this was the calm before the Christmas storm. One quiet night I noticed a thirty-something man over in the hunting section. Bored, I listened in on his conversation with the salesman.

"How'd you like the Arctic Cat ATV you bought?"

"Sweet. Goes anywhere. I went deer hunting last Saturday and bagged a stag."

"Great! So what can I do for you this time?"

"One of the guys I hunt with used a crossbow. Said it was more sporting."

"Well, it is more challenging. Maybe you should try it." The salesman took out an expensive crossbow and demonstrated how easy it was to use. "Just attach the bow to this pulley. Reels in just like a fishing rod. Put in an arrow, aim, and release. This model uses twenty-inch arrows."

"How much is it?"

"The bow's $500. You can get the whole package for just $699."

"Whew boy! My wife will kill me. The ATV set me back almost eight grand."

"Up to you, but I don't let *my* wife dictate," the salesman said.

What a jerk! Maybe Baldy had said the same thing when he sold Joe the boat. I wondered if they shared their techniques. Coming from another guy, the remark about the wife hit home like high school peer pressure, and the male customers succumbed.

"Wrap it up," the customer said. "If she complains, I'll just tell her she bought my Christmas present early."

"Great! I'll have to tell the other guys that excuse when they come in to buy." He made the customer's comment sound as brilliant as Einstein's equations.

Disgusted, I left a few minutes early for my dinner break. The weather was mild, so I pulled a beach chair from my trunk and swabbed my hands with the packaged bleach wipes I kept there. In my low chair on the edge of the ATV lot, I was practically invisible—always my preference especially when I'd heard something like tonight's nauseating crossbow sale.

As I bit into my sandwich, I heard the customer and the salesman out back testing the new toy on our demonstration targets. The salesman fell all over himself praising his customer's skill. Sickened by their banter, I stopped eating and lit up a cigarette. Eventually the salesman went inside, but I could still hear the *thunk* of the crossbow arrows hitting the target.

The headlights of a car whirled around the lot. I heard the driver pull into a spot and cut the engine. A few seconds later, the headlights blacked out, and a door slammed. The sound of high heels crossed the lot. A woman wearing a business suit emerged, walking near me. Just off work, I presumed. In the gathering dark, she didn't spot me until she was almost on top of me. She hesitated.

Even though I was on break, out of habit, I asked, "Can I help you?"

"I doubt if anyone can help me." Her voice sounded ragged and resigned.

"Why?"

"My lousy husband is addicted to this store. People talk about women spending money shopping, but compare women's closets to the gear stuffed into men's garages. They're the shopaholics."

"You're preaching to the choir, honey," I said. "My husband was a selfish bastard, too. You'd better head off yours before he spends more."

"Yeah, that's why I'm here. I'd bet the down payment on our house he's here looking at new hunting equipment. We're damn close to losing the house anyway." She looked straight ahead at the store as if assessing a battlefield.

Just then, the crossbow customer strolled across the parking lot, holding his bagged purchase and admiring the ATVs along the edge of the lot, as if the one he had bought wasn't enough. When the woman saw him, she took off, her heels clacking with speed and intensity as she approached him.

"Evan!"

"Jackie, what are you doing here?"

"Checking up on you, that's what."

"Who do you think you are, my mommy?" He turned to face her.

So the crossbow customer was her husband, I surmised. Poor woman.

"I can't believe you came back here after buying the ATV."

"Hey, you aren't the boss. I'll do what I want."

"You selfish bastard."

She'd used my own words, making me smile, and continued her tirade.

"After wiping out our savings on a stupid ATV, you're in here buying something else?"

"Yeah, I am. It will save us money." The customer opened his bag and pulled out his crossbow, fresh from the target range. The sales receipt fluttered to the ground, and the woman grabbed it.

She gasped and said, "$700. How will spending $700 save us money?"

"We can save on groceries when I bag more deer."

"You idiot! The kids won't even eat venison. How can you even try to justify spending money on yourself when we barely have money to buy Christmas presents for the kids?"

"You don't have to buy me a gift now. Let me show you how it works." He loaded an arrow and wound the pulley to ready the bow for firing, but his wife ignored his demonstration.

"Buy you a gift? Let me give you a reality check, Evan. I hadn't planned to give you a gift. We just have enough to buy a few clothes for the kids. We're behind on our mortgage payments. Give me that thing. I'm taking it back right now."

"The hell you are!"

They struggled, and she succeeded in pulling the crossbow out of her husband's hands. Unsteady from its weight, she turned it around to balance it. The arrow shot out of the crossbow and hit her husband in the chest. He immediately crumpled to the ground.

She reared back and blinked. I ran over and yanked the crossbow from her hands.

"Oh, my God, is he dead?" She stared at him, frozen.

I leaned over and checked his pulse. "Looks like the arrow went right through his heart. He's not breathing."

"I didn't mean to kill him. It just went off." She put her hands over her eyes, as if she couldn't bear seeing him. Her shoulders heaved, and her breathing came in gulps.

Putting my free hand on her shoulder, I told her the truth. "Doesn't matter, honey. A jury will decide whether you meant to kill him or not. His ATV purchase could be reason enough for them to convict you when they realize you're behind on your mortgage payments. Money's a common motive for murder. Now get out of here. No one will know."

She looked at me in disbelief. "You're kidding?"

"I'm dead serious. With your husband gone, your children will need you more than ever, so go on. Get!" I knew because my daughter was now a struggling single mother.

She hesitated. "You'll cover for me?"

"Honey, I've been in your shoes and feel your pain. Now get out of here. Don't speed. Just get in your car, go home to your children, and wait for the police to call you. You weren't here and will be shocked to hear about your husband's accident. Don't volunteer anything. If they question the accident, reluctantly claim that he was upset and despondent about your finances."

Narrowing her eyes, she focused, clearly understood my reasoning, and then looked around the parking lot and at the storefront. Both were empty. "Thank you," she said, and left.

I watched her car disappear down the road, then scurried to open my car trunk and put on the gloves I kept there. I grabbed the package of bleach wipes and obliterated any fingerprints on the crossbow.

Looking around, I hurried back to the husband. The lot was still empty. This would work. Once the husband loaded the arrow, he could have turned the crossbow around and hit the pulley release accidentally. Or even on purpose. I bent down and placed the crossbow backward into the man's hands, pressing his lifeless fingers around the bow and on the pulley release so he looked like the total idiot he was.

I stashed my gloves and wipes in my trunk, then repositioned my beach chair between the cars so I had no view of the ATVs. When the police arrived, I could easily say I didn't see anything.

When Joe died, I was lucky. I told his doctor how he grabbed his left arm before keeling over. Given Joe's heart condition, which his physician had been treating, attributing Joe's death to a heart attack was no problem. After his physician said Joe's heart attack wasn't surprising, the authorities hadn't performed an autopsy.

Joe had no remorse about wiping out my grandchildren's college fund, so I'd had no remorse about lacing his nightly bourbon and soda with some extra doses of his heart medication. If they had done an autopsy, I'd have blamed his suicidal overdose on his ProTrout spending spree. I was prepared to tell them how distraught he'd become about his inability to control his spending. But I was lucky.

I didn't need those explanations. Passing on my luck to that young mother, who had also reeled in a dud for a husband, seemed like the right thing to do.

And this time, without Joe, my college-savings plan for my granddaughters would work.

An author and beach bum of note, E. B. Davis writes short stories and novels in the mystery and paranormal-mystery genres. After graduating with a master's degree from George Washington University, she continued to degrade her writing skills working as a government-contractor analyst and as a construction manager. When she is not writing or blogging, she can be found at the beach, the setting for many of her stories. She is a member of the Short Mystery Fiction Society and Sisters in Crime. She blogs at http://writerswhokill.blogspot.com. Look for another of her stories, "Daddy's Little Girl," at http://voicesfromthegarage.com/story/daddys-little-girl.

MURDER BY MEDIATION
by Jill Breslau

Rainey drummed her fingertips on the polished conference table. She looked at the clock on the wall, and then at her watch, as if that would make a difference. Her mediation partner and their clients were all late. She drummed some more, listening to the soft click of her nails against the wood, and then glancing at her right hand. The French manicure looked perfect. Actually, she thought, leaning forward to admire her crossed legs, the shoes were perfect, too—expensive cobalt blue leather with four-inch heels. They matched her silk blouse and looked stunning with her classic black, barely knee-length suit.

Her own admiration was appropriate, she thought, unlike the sleazy admiration of certain judges she knew. When she'd been a trial lawyer, before she discovered mediation, one judge actually told her in open court that he couldn't hear what she was saying because he was so busy looking at her great legs. She wanted to use one of those great legs to kick him, hard, but she smiled sweetly and said, "Your Honor, I hope that isn't true, because we're on the record here, and I've just offered Document Eleven into evidence." She liked to look good, but she detested the cloying, hypersexual way that some men interpreted her style.

Lawrence, her mediation partner, was different. He was a truly nice man with good boundaries—and a great ass, thanks to all his bicycling. The thought popped into her mind unbidden, and she crushed it quickly, like squashing a bug, with a brisk reminder to herself: *And a wife and two children*. Cute, short, round-faced. He wasn't really her type, anyway.

She looked at the clock again. Usually Lawrence arrived promptly for their pre-session meeting to make sure they were on the same page, tuned in about the agenda. They had been a team since they'd heard of divorce mediation. It worked well for them, Rainey, who had been a tough litigator, and Lawrence, a social worker. Lawrence was gentler, more relaxed; Rainey was crisp, organized, and thorough. She enjoyed the intellectual quest for common ground as much as she had enjoyed skewering witnesses on the stand, which was saying something.

The door opened and one of the clients, Henry Linnet, stuck his head in. "Hi, Rainey. If they aren't here yet, I'll just pop into the little boys' room."

Rainey nodded and smiled, though she felt a spike of annoyance whenever adult males referred to the "little boys' room." *For God's sake, do they ever grow up?*

"Fine, Henry," she said.

Henry's wife, Barbara, and Lawrence still hadn't arrived when Henry returned. He sat in the swivel chair across from Rainey, gripped the table edge, and leaned forward, frowning. His wispy brown hair was disheveled, as if he'd been running his fingers through it. He wore a Hawaiian shirt, as usual, and the buttons strained across his chubby torso. Rainey had privately agreed with Lawrence that wearing Hawaiian shirts was probably the most daring thing Henry had ever done.

"Rainey, can I speak to you in confidence?"

She shrugged. "Everything in mediation is confidential, Henry, unless it has to do with abuse or anticipated violence."

"No, this isn't about that. This is about Barbara." He paused, and his eyes widened, as his head bobbed affirmatively. "I can't shake the feeling that she's having an affair."

Rainey's eyebrows lifted. "Barbara?"

"Don't be deceived by her demeanor, Rainey. She may look sweet and bland, but she has a wild, passionate streak."

Rainey struggled to keep the disbelief off her face. Barbara was the least sexy woman she had ever met. She had flat brown eyes, light brown hair, the same color as her husband's, and very small, white teeth that looked as if she'd never lost her baby teeth. She spoke in a girlish, breathy voice, like Marilyn Monroe. Unlike Marilyn, she wore long, baggy earth-tone-colored skirts and loose tops that she didn't tuck in, as if she had done all her clothes shopping sometime in the '60s. Rainey referred to her privately, and to Lawrence, as "Miss Mouse."

"What makes you think she's having an affair?"

Henry frowned again and looked at her. "She's too happy. We're in a divorce. We're arguing about custody of the children. We've got to divide up all our property, and she won't have as much money as she's used to. She's going to have to start tutoring, as well as teaching, to make the budget work. But she's happy, almost giddy."

He paused and then continued, "And she's coming on to me all the time."

"She is?"

"It's confusing."

"So, Henry, are you sleeping with her?"

"Are you kidding? Of course I am."

Rainey felt a rush of disgust that twitched the corners of her mouth downward. She looked away, hoping he was too self-absorbed to have noticed.

"But you think there's someone else, too?" Rainey crossed her arms as he nodded again, and then she leaned back in her chair. "Well, how can I help you?"

"I don't know. I guess I just wanted to tell somebody. And I wanted to know if it's a legal problem."

"Maryland's only a no-fault state if people can swear they've lived apart for a year before a divorce, without cohabitation. That means without sleeping together. So every time you sleep together after separation, you push the date for a divorce back. Does that make sense?"

"Yeah. Well, I don't want the divorce, anyway, so if it takes longer, that's fine by me."

"Well, Henry, I'm not a therapist, and I can't second-guess your feelings. But from a legal perspective, Maryland allows adultery as grounds for divorce, so if Barbara is having an affair, you could get into court whenever you want on those grounds." Rainey had repeated similar words so many times in her career, they rolled out automatically.

Henry nodded. One side of his mouth twisted in a wry smile. "I can't prove anything. It just seems strange to me, her mood."

Rainey leaned forward, encouragingly. "Henry, divorce is difficult. It hits people different ways. Don't jump to conclusions."

While she spoke, she noticed his gaze falling to her cleavage, and she sat straighter in her chair. It had been annoying enough to be the object of sexist remarks in the courtroom, but in her own conference room? She took a deep breath and set her jaw tightly.

There was a knock on the door, and Barbara opened it without waiting for an invitation. Rainey glanced at her watch. Twenty minutes late. And where was Lawrence?

Barbara settled herself in a chair, swiveling toward Rainey. "I'm sorry to be late. Something came up." Then a red flush made its way from her neck up to her forehead. It made Rainey wonder if breasts could blush. Maybe Henry was right. Maybe Barbara was having an affair.

"It's all right. Lawrence isn't here yet," Rainey said, "and I haven't heard from him…" The door opened again.

"I apologize," Lawrence said. He was red-faced and out of breath. "I had some bike problems. I'll be just a moment more; I need some water."

As he left the room, Barbara gazed after him as if he were something edible. Rainey watched the expression on Barbara's face. She sighed. Lawrence had counseled Barbara before she decided to divorce Henry, and then he changed hats, so to speak, and brought the couple into mediation. Rainey had learned it could be a pain to work in mediation with clients Lawrence had seen before as a therapist; their therapeutic transference and silly fantasies about Lawrence didn't make her job easier. Rainey began shuffling through the file, and Lawrence came back, holding a water glass, his hair damp around his face. As he reached across the table to shake hands with Henry, Rainey glimpsed Barbara's expression. Her adoring look warped briefly, her upper lip curling in a silent hiss.

"Are we all ready to begin the session?" Rainey asked, taking control.

They began discussing parenting arrangements for Henry and Barbara's two young children. Barbara hadn't wanted to share custody, claiming they were too young; Henry, however, was terrified of losing his children. He fretted about whether his relationship with them would be healthy if he saw them infrequently, and he wasn't reassured by Rainey's assertion that he would always be their father. Then, to Rainey's surprise, Barbara suddenly turned to Henry and said, "You know, I've been wrong. You're a good dad, and you deserve to have the children half the time."

Rainey found herself moved by Barbara's acknowledgement of her husband. A tear darted to her eye, followed swiftly by a thought darting through her head. *Sure, more time with the lover if Henry's got the kids.*

At the end of the session, Barbara and Henry left together, closing the door behind them. Lawrence grinned at Rainey.

"Good job, partner!"

He jumped up and headed for the door. Rainey frowned. Usually they debriefed their sessions, but maybe he needed to fix the bike? She caught a whiff of a sweaty, musky scent as he dashed out of the office, jogging toward the bicycle he always parked at a meter on the curb. The bike still had the little buggy attached that he had used to cart his children around when they were small. Five years later, he said it worked fine for carrying groceries home, even though the kids had outgrown it.

She watched him cycle away, still vaguely charmed by his refusal to drive a car (his environmental statement, he said), his involvement in transporting his children, and his willingness to go food shopping, before she turned back to the conference room. She was less charmed by the sweat that came with the cycling. Nevertheless, he'd done a lot to grow this business, she thought. It wouldn't have happened without him. As she tucked her notes in the file, gathered coffee cups from the conference room table, and ran a cloth saturated with furniture polish over the table top, familiar images ran through her head. Pre-Lawrence, and pre-mediation, her life had been a series of infuriating events:

Rainey standing outside a courtroom, breathing deeply to lower the register of her voice. She'd realized early on that the good-ol'-boy judges tuned out their wives' voices and, thus, the voices of women lawyers. If she didn't speak in a deep voice, she literally wasn't heard.

Rainey, during a party, pushing open an unlocked bathroom door in the fancy home of a big-firm lawyer to discover one of the judges snorting cocaine. Great, a cokehead was making vital decisions about people's lives.

Rainey, coming up the courthouse inside stairwell to beg a judicial assistant for hearing time, since the judge she had been scheduled to appear before had canceled the day's docket. Then, seeing that same judge rushing down the stairs, his robe billowing around him to disclose white tennis shorts. Clearly, he couldn't wait to get out of the courthouse and onto the courts.

She had first been disappointed and then disgusted that these shallow, sexist, selfish men were making decisions that changed people's lives forever. She hated being in a courtroom where they held the power. She had complained bitterly to her friends. And it was her friend Lawrence who called her one day, excited, to tell her about a brand new concept for divorcing couples called mediation, where couples worked together to find shared values and common ground. They had rushed out to California for training and set up their business. Their slogan was simple, but they believed it: "Finding Win-Win Solutions!"

Rainey chuckled to herself, remembering their talks to the ministerial association, the local psychologists, and anyone else who would listen. Even professionals were so clueless that they thought Rainey and Lawrence were coming to teach them mediTAtion, not mediAtion. Coincidentally, after observing Rainey's short fuse (wasn't he kind to call it that, instead of an "anger management issue"?), Lawrence taught her mediTAtion. Sometimes they would sit together, breathing quietly, until her jaws relaxed and her shoulders eased.

Given the number of daily aggravations she faced, Rainey ended up meditating a lot.

* * * *

Work continued for the next week, at its usual pace. Sessions, agreements, and then Henry and Barbara were due to come in for another appointment.

Henry called a few hours before their scheduled time, sounding strained. "Rainey, I've got to cancel. Barbara has to go out of town to see her parents; they're old, and she's worried about them."

"You sound tense or sarcastic or something. Are you?"

"I don't know. I think she might be stalling about equal custody—buyer's remorse or whatever. She made a commitment, and now she's looking for ways to pretend she didn't."

"Henry," Rainey said, "I don't think you need to worry. You both seemed to be working in good faith, and Barbara agreed that the two of you would share time with the children equally. Shall we schedule for next week and focus on the last details then?"

Henry agreed, though he clearly was worried.

"I'll speak to Barbara," he said, "and I'll let you know if there's a problem. Otherwise, same day, same time, next week."

The day before their next appointment, Henry called again.

"Rainey, I don't know whether Barbara's coming tomorrow or not. I kind of lost it when she got back from visiting her parents in Chicago."

"You lost it? What happened?"

"Awww. You know, it was a hard week taking care of the kids alone. They were acting out and whining for Mommy, and Barbara didn't call when she said she would." He paused.

"So?"

"So she came in all bubbly and giggly, while I was putting dinner on the table, as if she'd spent the day drinking champagne instead of dragging luggage through airports after a downer visit with her parents. I told her I knew she was having an affair. Well, I kind of yelled at her in front of the kids. Then I said, 'Tell me who it is!' and she looked at me as if I was a worm, and she shifted gears completely from the happy, bubbly mood and said, very coldly, 'You are scum to suggest that.' She started to walk away, and I threw the mac-and-cheese casserole at the wall."

"Did you throw it at her?"

"No, I just got so mad, I threw it at the dining room wall. It didn't even splatter on her. And I cleaned it all up myself and took the kids out to eat."

"So…is there a problem?"

"I'm afraid to ask her if she's coming to tomorrow's appointment. Will you call her?"

"Sure. Assume it's on unless I call you back to the contrary."

Thank God Henry couldn't see her face. The thought of mild-mannered, dull Henry flinging a dish of mac and cheese at the wall had made her grin.

When she called Barbara, Rainey asked if they could work things out. Barbara said yes, that she had been relieved to get away, and she knew Henry had been stressed staying home, and he had misunderstood the cause of her euphoria.

"I couldn't exactly tell him I was just ecstatic to have been out of his presence, could I?"

"Not really," Rainey agreed. "But, Barbara, if there is someone else important in your life, Henry might be intuiting the presence of what we call a 'ghost' at the mediation table. You know, someone who isn't there but whose presence is somehow making a difference."

"There is no ghost at the table," Barbara said in a firm voice, unlike her usual Marilyn Monroe whisper.

Rainey called Lawrence and told him all about the conversations, including the fact that Henry thought Miss Mouse had a lover (and wasn't that a hoot?).

"Lori," he said, "Give it a rest. Let's just get this one done, okay?"

What was his problem? He never called her Lori, the other derivative of her given name, Lorraine, unless he was annoyed. He knew she hated the name.

"Okay, Larry," she snapped back, emphasizing the *Larry*. She knew Lawrence thought it made him sound like a youngster, a light-weight, rather than a professional.

But when he arrived for their sessions the next morning, they were a team, as usual. They had a session with one of the local real estate moguls and his wife and sat chatting afterward about what the odds were that the husband didn't already have a girlfriend.

"Men never get out of marriages unless they have girlfriends, Lawrence. Haven't you noticed? It must be something psychological," Rainey said.

"Well, pal," Lawrence replied, "you might have noticed that a fair number of women have boyfriends on the back burner, too."

"Nope, it's not the same. Sometimes women leave a marriage just because it isn't working, not because of somebody else. But men—the only issue is whether they hide the girlfriend or the wife finds out."

The phone rang in the outer office, interrupting their conversation. Rainey went to pick it up and then transferred the call to the conference room and pressed the button for speakerphone. It was Arnold Eldridge, a former courtroom adversary. She knew Arnold all too well; he was a terrible lawyer, lacking in common sense, creating problems where none existed, just to flog the files and make more money. Worse, he was dismally unattractive, so there wasn't even the consolation of dealing with someone inept but cute. His thin hair stuck to his skull in a bad comb-over; his face was cratered from adolescent acne, and, in all seasons, he wore lumpy brown tweed suits. After numerous confrontations with him, Rainey started to seethe at the sound of his voice. She struggled to keep her own voice level and polite.

"Rainey," he began, and she interjected, "Arnold, I have Lawrence here in my office as well. I understand you now represent Barbara and are calling about today's appointment?"

"Rainey and Lawrence," he continued, with exaggerated courtesy, "I want to let you know that I have advised Barbara to discontinue mediation. Her husband got violent when she came back from visiting her elderly parents, and mediation is unsuitable in situations of domestic violence."

"Arnold," Rainey said, "I just spoke with Barbara yesterday. All Henry did was throw a dish of mac and cheese at the wall. That isn't domestic violence. They were making good progress in mediation."

"Rainey, I didn't call to argue with you. Barbara is my client now. I have had her husband served with a restraining order, which will keep him away from her and the children. We will be litigating this case. She will not be returning to mediation."

"Arnold, that's not a good idea," Rainey said, trying to reason with him. "Henry is terrified of losing his children, and he'll be very upset. They were doing so well in mediation until she took this trip. Can't you help us keep a lid on things and keep them in a process that's working?"

"He's a violent man," Arnold said flatly. "He needs to understand that the law will not permit that kind of behavior."

Oh, Lord, Rainey thought, and looked at Lawrence in utter frustration.

"Arnold," Lawrence said, "please tell Barbara that if she changes her mind and wants to come back into mediation, we'll be pleased to continue working with them."

After they hung up, Rainey was ready to beat her head against a wall; Lawrence seemed to take the situation more philosophically. He said he thought he'd use the time freed up by the canceled appointment to go grocery shopping. After he left the office, she watched him through the window. He pulled his bike away from the meter he had locked it to and pedaled away.

Rainey called Henry. "I'm so sorry this happened, Henry! I feel sure Barbara will figure out that Arnold isn't helpful, and you'll be fine. You did a lot of good work in mediation."

"Rainey, I can't believe he did this. Barbara goes away, I get upset, and now I've lost my kids?" Henry was distressed but fully coherent.

"No, no, Henry, you haven't lost them. It's a temporary setback."

Henry began to cry.

"Look, Henry, you have to obey the restraining order or things could get worse, and you need your own good lawyer now. Hire someone and listen to what she tells you."

"Can't you get Barbara back into mediation?"

"No, I wish I could. It's a voluntary process, and if she doesn't want to come back, no one can make her. Henry, did you hear me about getting your own lawyer?"

Henry reluctantly agreed.

Rainey was so discouraged that she couldn't face an evening alone at home, ruminating about lousy lawyers and the cases, and lives, they made more difficult. She ordered in dinner, and settled down to paperwork.

Which is why she was still in the office when Lawrence called around ten p.m.

Unlike Henry, her friend wasn't coherent. At least, she couldn't understand what he was saying. He'd gone to see Barbara, (their client, Barbara?), and something about four men, and the Chicago trip had been totally fabricated, and she'd been sick in bed for a week? No, that couldn't be what he said. Rainey told him to calm down and come to the office, and she'd make coffee.

She was watching for him when his bike wobbled down the street with its little headlight pushing away the darkness, and he climbed off and leaned it against the meter. He came in shaking, as if the weather outside were bitter and cold, instead of a balmy seventy degrees. Her desk was a mess, so she poured coffee for them both and took it into the conference room, pulled coasters out of the drawer, and set the mugs down in the usual ritual. Lawrence followed her like a dazed animal and sat at the table, his hands limp in his lap.

Then he got himself under control, looked her in the eye and said, "I've been having an affair with Barbara."

"Barbara?" Her voice rose. "Barbara, of Henry and Barbara? Barbara Linnet?"

He nodded his head, now looking down, the moment of confession turning to shame. "Don't say anything yet, Rainey. There's more."

She bit back the remarks on the tip of her tongue about professional ethics, the incredible damage he was doing to their collective reputations by sleeping with a client, the way he was destroying not only his own marriage but the business that was her identity, the business they had worked so hard together to build. She gritted her teeth, mastered the impulse to throw the coffee in his face, sighed loudly, and said, in her steeliest voice, "Go on."

"I knew Barbara's kids were spending the night with friends, so I went to see her tonight. I was worried about her hiring such a stupid, vicious lawyer. I thought it would backfire, you know, that he would drag out the divorce and make everything take forever."

"Lawrence, how long have you been sleeping with her?"

"Since after our first mediation session. I don't suppose you could tell that she kept rubbing my foot with hers under the table. Her hand…she had her hand on my thigh. You remember, when I nearly knocked the table over? It's funny, nothing happened when she was my therapy patient." He looked at Rainey, as if he actually thought she would remember and understand, or even approve of his restraint with a patient. "She was so hot, Rainey, I can't even tell you."

"Don't, Lawrence. Do not tell me. Stop right there." A surge of rage rolled from Rainey's gut to the top of her head. She could feel her cheeks burning, as if flames would pour out of her mouth if she opened it. *Hot,* she thought, *I'll show you hot!*

Lawrence's face turned very red, and she realized that he wasn't that cute when he blushed.

She took some calming breaths, then spoke slowly. "Lawrence, the other day, when you and Barbara were both late...?"

"Uh, yeah." He nodded. "We were together." A faint expression crossed his face that looked smug, self-satisfied, but it disappeared in a fraction of a second.

Then suddenly his face contorted, and he put his head down on the table and clutched at his stomach. "I killed her, Rainey."

"What in God's name are you talking about, Lawrence?"

"When she told me about Henry getting so mad, I made sure she had a gun in the house. I knew I was overreacting, but I couldn't help myself. I went over there tonight, and she told me I had betrayed her and she would never forgive me. She said she thought I was on her side until she saw me fawning over Henry. Rainey, you know that's not true! I'm neutral as a mediator, and I was just being professional and polite."

Rainey closed her eyes. Her jaw was locked, as she chose not to say what she was thinking: *Right, Lawrence! It's very polite and neutral to shake hands with a client whose wife you just got out of bed with. Good job!*

When she opened her eyes, Lawrence cleared his throat. "She told me she was sleeping with four different guys and I was the worst lay. She said she didn't go to Chicago, she went to the beach and spent most of the week in bed with one of them. And then she said Henry turned her on so much by throwing the macaroni dish that she was thinking of getting back together with him. She said"—at this point, Lawrence started to cry—"she said no matter how smart I am, I don't have a clue about sex. She ridiculed me, Rainey. I went to get the gun out of the drawer I'd put it in. Jeez, if she was going to make fun of me, I wasn't going to let her use my gun for protection. But when I picked it up…" He looked down at the table, shaking his head, bewildered. Then he faced Rainey again. "She jeered at me. She said, 'Oh, the gun, now that makes you a real man,' and it went off. It shot her."

It shot her?

He paused. "Rainey? You know I didn't mean to, don't you?"

He sounded like a little boy whose ball had just shattered his mother's favorite vase.

Rainey closed her eyes again for a few minutes, working her jaw to relax it, so she could speak. Then she said, "We both better calm down. Let's sit for a few minutes and meditate, and we'll figure out what to do."

Lawrence cried and cried. He was not cute at all.

Rainey sat with her eyes closed, inhaling, exhaling. Logical thoughts followed each other. The implications of Lawrence's disclosure weren't pretty. If he were caught, at best he'd wind up in prison for the rest of his life, his wife and the kids would be humiliated, and Rainey's legal reputation would be down the toilet. All those scornful lawyers who claimed mediation was just a ploy to avoid being a trial lawyer, all those jealous lawyers who envied her success, they'd be snickering about her forever. "Your partner kill any clients lately? Har, har, har." Her thriving business had just been annihilated.

Could she fix it? What if Lawrence claimed he was visiting Barbara as her therapist? She became overwhelmed with guilt about her promiscuity, threatened to shoot herself, and in the struggle for the gun, it went off?

Sure, that would work fine, except that Lawrence bought the gun. No story would fix that. No matter what else happened, Rainey was sure to get screwed now. *Damn. He'd seemed so different from every other idiot male she knew. How in hell could she control the damage?*

She opened her eyes.

"Did anyone else know you were seeing her? Did Sheila guess?"

"Absolutely not," he said. "I'm sure we were discreet, and Sheila would never suspect."

"Did anyone spot you going in or out of Barbara's house tonight?"

He paused. "I don't think so."

"What did you do with the gun?" she asked.

"I wiped it down and brought it with me."

"What?" Her voice rose to nearly a screech.

"I'll be right back."

She stood at the window, looking at him as he hurried toward his bike in its usual spot under the street lamp. He leaned into the enclosure behind the bike, pulled out a grocery bag, and headed back in. *He's absolutely lost it. He left the gun in the bike carriage?* Moments later, Lawrence gave her the bag, which contained a solid object wrapped in bathroom tissue, and she put it into her office safe while he watched her.

"I'll dispose of it later," she said. "Okay, Lawrence, wash your face and go home to your family. Say nothing. Surely the cops will try to pin it on Henry, and he'll have an alibi, and they'll be left with a cold case. You'll be fine."

She paused, took a slow breath, and nodded with assurance. "I'm going to follow you to your house to make sure you get there safely."

When she pulled her Lexus SUV around from the parking lot behind the building, the headlights illuminated Lawrence waiting in the street beside his bicycle. He jumped on and began pedaling, and she thought she could see the muscles flexing in the once-cute ass under his khakis. She kept him in her headlights as he gained speed on the dark highway, cycling fast, as if trying to outrun his thoughts.

In contrast, Rainey wasn't thinking, for once. Shell-shocked and exhausted, she watched her business partner's dark head bobbing in front of her as he pumped the pedals. No cars passed in either direction on the dark road, but still she focused on driving, her jaw clenched, intent on maintaining just the right distance.

Rainey followed Lawrence all the way to the right turn that would take him home, the road that swept down the hillside in sharp curves before reaching his narrow driveway. He might have success-fully made the turn if she hadn't sped up beside him and edged him to the sandy shoulder of the road. He might still have made the turn if she hadn't then braked to clip, just barely, the carriage trailing behind him. But she did both those things, simultaneously turning her headlights off and on, off and on. At speed, unable to see in the intermittent flashes of light, he skidded out of control on the sand and slammed into the concrete retaining wall next to the roadway.

Rainey stopped the car, turned her headlights off, and waited a minute in the car, taking deep breaths. *Did it work?* Kicking off her elegant heels, she grabbed a flashlight from the glove box and got out of the car. She trained her flashlight on the body crumpled beside the road. His head was twisted at an unnatural angle, and his chest didn't show even a whisper of movement.

Then she sighed a deep sigh of relief and regret.

"Larry," she said, shaking her head, "Larry. Damned if you didn't turn out to be a Larry. For all these years, I thought you were a Lawrence. I've put up with your being cute and unavailable. I could handle your being married, and I even like your wife. But killing a client is way out of line. It's bad for our reputation, so not good for business. Dammit, Larry, you made it a lose-lose! You brought this on yourself."

She walked back to the car, turning back one time. "And if you were going to screw around," she shook her head again. "Oh, Larry. Miss Mouse?"

Jill Breslau is a lawyer and psychotherapist who has, indeed, worked as a divorce mediator. The major incidents in this story are unrelated to her actual experience. Some of the less dramatic events are true, though it's to no one's advantage to identify them. Jill lives in Maryland with her golden retriever, Mr. Jones. She has four adorable grandchildren who may find it difficult to imagine, when they grow up, that their grandmother could write about people who have wicked thoughts and do terrible things. She has written legal articles; this is her first short story.

DEADRISE
by David Autry

Plunging into the cold water of the Chesapeake Bay jolted me awake. Fear and panic overwhelmed me. I gasped for air as the boat sped off into the darkness. The last thing I remembered before hitting the water was a kaleidoscope exploding in my head. Someone on the boat had hit me from behind before dumping me overboard.

My chest heaved as brackish water washed into my lungs. My arms and legs felt like lead. On the verge of passing out, I swam toward a small green light swaying back and forth in the choppy water. I was determined to survive. I had a score to settle.

* * * *

Brief snatches of my ordeal and rescue flitted through my sluggish brain as warm sunlight and the smell of fresh coffee began to revive me. I opened one eye. The digital clock on a bedside table read 9:05. I ached. The pain in my head pulsed. My throat was dry, and my eyelids felt like sandpaper. The room faded in and out of focus. I shut my eyes and counted to ten. When I opened them again, a lanky, weathered man stood over me. I guessed he was around seventy.

I felt woozy but strong enough to sit up. The covers were damp, and I felt a sudden chill as I swung my bare legs over the side of the bed.

"I'm washing your clothes, son, and you could sure use a shower," the old man said, putting a cup of coffee and a bowl of soup on the bedside table. "I thought you might want something to eat." He helped me into a faded blue terrycloth bathrobe.

The broth was warm and soothing, and my strength began to return. As I ate, he told me how he'd seen me clinging to a navigation buoy bobbing in the bay. "It must have taken all your will to survive. I thought it best to bring you home with me."

"Where am I?"

"Piney Point."

"I can't thank you enough, mister..." I almost choked on the broth.

"Newhouse, Bill Newhouse, and you're Shelby Reid. I saw your ID when I spread the things in your wallet out to dry. I'm pleased to meet you, Shelby, and you're welcome." He offered me a large, work-roughened hand with long, square-tipped fingers.

Clean clothes were on the bed when I finished my shower. "You had only one sock on when we pulled you out of the bay," Newhouse said from the other room. "Come on in and we'll get you fixed up."

"We?" Tucking in my shirttail, I stopped in the doorway, wondering who else was in the house.

"Mr. Reid, this is my niece, Denise. She's visiting for the weekend, as she often does. Join us for coffee." He gestured toward a cushioned chair, identical to one occupied by a woman in her early thirties, about my age. Tall and athletic with a generous, friendly smile, she stood to greet me.

"Denise and I like to take my boat out early in the morning to watch the birds and other inhabitants of the bay. It's really spectacular, and we never know what we'll find out there," the old man said.

I took that as my cue to explain how I came to be in their debt.

I made up a story about fishing with some guys I met in a bar. "The three of us were on this fancy, new cabin cruiser, drinking and swapping fish tales. Then the owner said something about his buddy's ex-wife, and they started arguing," I said. "When the owner accused the other guy of sleeping with his wife, things got nasty.

"They were pretty drunk," I continued, "and things got out of hand. They started fighting like a couple of kids, and I tried to get in between them. That's when one of them punched me, and I hit my head and fell into the water. Don't think either of them noticed, they were going at it so hard."

My rescuers looked at one another, then back at me.

"Maybe I should call the cops and tell them what happened," I said, setting my cup down.

"In a sense, you already have," the old man said. "My niece is a sergeant with the Maryland Natural Resources Police."

Denise Newhouse smoothed back an errant strand of dark auburn hair, and her wide-set brown eyes narrowed as she asked, "Do you want to press charges against your fishing buddies?"

I felt a wave of panic in the pit of my stomach. "No, don't think so. Hell, I don't even remember their names. Besides, it was pretty stupid of me to get on that boat with a couple of strangers in the first place."

Later Denise drove me to the bar in Solomons where I'd left my car. We barely spoke on the ride through the Southern Maryland countryside. Every so often a lonely farm house or the skeleton of a tree intruded on the open fields, still brown from the winter's frosts and snow.

We said our goodbyes, and I promised to return the sneakers her uncle let me borrow. On the drive back to my apartment in Baltimore, I pondered my next move.

I'd spent months tracking the cocaine trade from small-time street dealers to their suppliers, and I wanted to go all the way up the food chain and get the whole story. But all I had come up with so far was a busted head and a pair of borrowed sneakers. What I needed was a different approach.

* * * *

Thanks to a crash course in undercover work from a cop friend, I eventually was able to pass myself off as an ex-convict looking for some easy money. Over the course of the next three months, I learned a lot about the drug business and could even tell the weight of a gram of coke just by feel. But the hardest part was keeping up with the constantly changing street lingo. It's not just the names for all the drugs, but I had to know the latest slang for everything from the quantity and price of drugs to ordering a drink. A bartender can hang a jacket on an undercover man faster than anyone.

I got to know most of the dealers and suppliers in Baltimore and bought enough of their wares to convince them I wasn't a narc—I hoped.

I was just leaving my apartment one chilly night when a supplier named Whitey came up behind. "Word is you're looking for a payday," he said in a coarse whisper. "But, hey, ain't we all? Let's pull in here for something to warm us up."

Whitey was about forty years old, blond, and watchful. He had a ruthless reputation that kept his street dealers in line. If anyone ever crossed him, there wouldn't be a second time.

Even though the weather was cold and windy, sweat ran down the back of my neck as we entered the Komoto Club. I tried to remember anything that might have made Whitey suspicious. Had someone recognized me from my days as a reporter with the old *Washington Tribune*?

The Komoto was a favorite hangout among Baltimore's criminal element. Whitey steered me to a corner table in the rear and ordered us both a double Jack Daniels. We waited in silence until the bartender delivered our drinks.

"Yo, what do you know about boats and shit like that?"

Whitey's question caught me by surprise. That kind of casual conversation just doesn't happen in the drug world. Strictly business and that's it. There's an unwritten law about not asking questions, and no one offers any information about themselves.

I took a thoughtful sip of my drink before telling him I'd worked on a charter boat out of Annapolis before ending up in the state prison at Jessup.

Whitey's eyes scanned the dimly lit bar for anyone who might be close enough to overhear and leaned toward me. "I got what you might call a situation," he said. "And maybe you could help me out and do yourself some good at the same time." He paused. "You know a big supplier named Sketcher?"

I tried to look indifferent even as my heart rate accelerated. But Whitey's words had triggered a small earthquake under my chair. I reached for my glass, barely able to keep my hand from jerking as I bent to take a drink. Then I shook my head.

"Well, me and him did business together for a few years, until he got greedy and got himself paid off for good," Whitey said. "Now I got a shot at taking over his operation, and I need somebody who knows about boats to help me move stuff up the bay."

Sketcher had been one of the area's biggest wholesalers in the drug trade, and I'd tried to get close to him for a long time. He was to have been an unwitting key source for my exposé on dope smuggling in the bay area, but that hadn't worked out. Maybe Whitey's ambition to move up was the break I needed.

* * * *

Three days later, Whitey and I drove to St. Mary's County in Southern Maryland. I rented a waterman's cottage on St. George Island, a tiny, two-square-mile community with a few dozen residents. Whitey checked into a motel in Leonardtown where he introduced me to a couple of small-time crooks who had worked for Sketcher a few years back. Whitey explained that when a drug shipment came up the Chesapeake, my job was to collect the drugs by boat and wait at my place for him to come get it. I'd be well paid for one night's work about twice a month.

Whitey said it would take a couple of weeks to get things set up. He drove back to Baltimore. I began searching the want ads for a used boat, something that wouldn't draw too much attention.

On my way to look at boats, I drove across the causeway to Piney Point so I could return Bill Newhouse's sneakers. He seemed glad to see me again, and over coffee told me where I could get a good deal on an old deadrise workboat.

Next day I took delivery. The previous owner, Newhouse told me, built the forty-foot craft in 1949 and used it to dredge oysters and harvest crabs for nearly sixty years. The boat was powered by a government-surplus GM six-cylinder diesel engine still in good shape, but her wooden hull and decking needed some work. I renamed her the *Lady Janette* and set about making repairs and repainting. I wish it had been so easy to patch up her namesake.

I was washing out paint brushes one sunny afternoon when Whitey called. A shipment of cocaine was coming up the Chesapeake that night and would be stashed in a duck blind along the southern shore of Taylor Cove. My first job.

I put the *Lady J* through her paces getting to know the area, located the drop point, then headed home for supper. About three in the morning, I took the *Lady J* out again. Even though the night was clear with a nearly full moon, I had a hard time finding the cache anchored among the reeds and grasses along the shore. The duck blind was an eight-foot flat-bottomed boat with a camouflaged pop-up canopy that blended in with its surroundings. It was an ingenious set-up with a whisper-quiet electric motor so it could be moved from one secluded spot to another.

I hefted the duffle bag from the blind into the *Lady J* and headed back to my cottage. I covered my illicit cargo with a tarp and some coils of rope and brewed a pot of strong coffee. Whitey was supposed to meet me and take the drugs to a stash house, but by late morning he hadn't shown. If something went wrong, I sure didn't want to be left holding a load of coke worth millions.

Repeated phone calls to Whitey went unanswered, so I decided to examine the duffle bag's contents. Instead of cocaine, I found about forty plastic-wrapped packets of powdered chalk like the stuff used to mark boundaries and baselines on athletic fields. Was this a test to see if I could be trusted or was Whitey being double crossed? Either way, I was in a fix.

I couldn't think what else to do, so I decided to stay in character and act the part of a pissed-off ex-con. I waited until ten o'clock at night and put the duffle bag in the trunk of my car then drove to a roadside bar where Whitey and his crew often went.

I pulled into the parking lot and backed my Honda up to Whitey's Mercedes convertible. The afternoon had been unusually warm, and he'd left the car's top down. I took the bag from my trunk, ripped it open with my seaman's knife, and emptied the contents into Whitey's front seat. I took a few minutes to work up my nerve and stomped into the roadhouse like I had a chip on my shoulder as big as a railroad tie.

I spotted my quarry at the bar with his back to me. I scanned the shabby, dimly lit room for Whitey's thugs and didn't see them. I made straight for Whitey, grabbed his shoulder with my left hand, and spun him around on the stool to face me. I drew my right arm back, making a tight fist, and unleashed a roundhouse punch that landed solidly on the startled man's jaw. My hand hurt like hell. I stepped back and let him get up so he'd know who had clocked him. He recovered quicker than I expected and tried to tackle me on the run. I landed three or four hard blows on his head and shoulders before we both crashed to the rancid, beer-spattered floor. I rolled out from under him and started to push myself up on one knee when I felt a jolt on the back of my head, and that kaleidoscope exploded again.

* * * *

The still night air was clammy and cool when I came to, slumped against a rusty wire fence on the edge of an open field. Along with the smell of damp earth, I caught the distinctive odor of a chicken-processing plant. My head and shoulders complained as I struggled into a lopsided sitting position. With my hands tied behind me around a wobbly wooden fence post, I banged my back against the pole until I could pull it out of the ground. I worked my bound hands down the roughened wood, wincing as splinters dug into my forearms.

Savoring my small triumph, I rested, listening to the night. The flutter of an owl's wings and a rustle among the dead leaves nearby sent a shiver up my spine.

I maneuvered my arms under my butt and pulled my legs and feet through the loop so my hands were in front. I untied the rope with my teeth. After my head cleared, I stood and willed my shaky legs to carry me toward a murky glow in the distance. Somewhere along the way I'd lost my cell phone, so I walked to a gas station and called the first person I could think of to come get me.

Bill Newhouse answered the phone, but it was his niece who picked me up. Back at my cottage, she dug out splinters and cleaned and patched my cuts.

"I figured we'd cross paths again," she said. "You should know, I didn't believe that bull about drunk fishing buddies, so I did some checking. And guess what? Not only did nobody report you missing, you're a reporter for *Inside Access* magazine, and you love the big story." She leaned in. "Well, I love the big story, too, though for other reasons. I've been keeping my eye on you the last few months, waiting. Now here's our chance."

Our chance?

Sergeant Denise Newhouse, I soon learned, was not just a game warden. In one of those wild, you're-not-gonna-believe-this coincidences, she was assigned to Maryland's High Intensity Drug Unit. HIDU, as it is called, was set up to investigate and prevent drug trafficking on the Chesapeake Bay and its tributaries. When I had recovered from my shock, I figured she had a right to know that I was tracking the cocaine trade in the Baltimore-Washington area for my magazine. I told her one of my sources had arranged for me to meet a distributor named Sketcher the night she and her uncle rescued me. I'd driven to a bar in Solomons where two muscle-bound guys with shaved heads took me outside and searched me. When a white Ford van pulled up, one of the baldy twins jammed a hood over my head and—with little apparent effort—lifted me into the back.

"After a torturous, suffocating ride, I was ushered aboard a swanky cabin cruiser that was supposed to take me to Sketcher," I told Denise. "We were pretty far off shore when one of my escorts got a call on his cell phone. Next thing I knew somebody hit me from behind and dumped me over the side."

"So, you were supposed to meet Sketcher?" Denise's gaze shifted from me to the floor. "Word is he got caught holding out on his customers, taking an extra cut for himself," she said. "He and three of his associates were found in a warehouse. Each one had been shot execution style and had a hundred-dollar bill stuffed in his mouth."

I'd expected as much after my meeting with Whitey at the Komoto Club.

"You should know that a guy named Whitey had taken over Sketcher's operation, and I've got a job in his organization; or at least I did," I said.

"Look, if you had any sense you'd walk away from this before you get killed. No job is worth your life," she said.

"Can't do it. It's not just a job; this is personal. I owe it to somebody to shine the light on those cockroaches so the cops can stomp them out."

I told her about my best friend's daughter who died of a drug overdose. Her name was Janette, and she was bright and full of life. She'd been an honors student at Johns Hopkins University until her drug habit took control. She ended up selling her books, her car, and herself just to get high.

"It was the worst day of my life seeing her thin, drug-ravaged body in the morgue, and I had to break the news to her dad," I said. "I felt empty and powerless. So at her funeral I made a promise to do everything possible to keep someone else's son or daughter from dying that way."

"So, is it some kind of revenge or vigilante justice you're after? Because if it is, I'll have to arrest you for your own good." Denise poured peroxide on a nasty gouge in my arm and asked what I planned to do.

The medicine stung, and I gritted my teeth. "All I want is to get at the truth about the drug traffic and maybe find a better way to fight it. For years the government's said they're making headway against drugs. But my sources at the Drug Enforcement Administration say all this so-called success hasn't put a dent in the drug trade. More dope than ever is on our streets, and it's killing people every day. Something's got to be done to stop it," I said.

I told Denise about Whitey's drug-smuggling operation and my part in it. After a pause she said, "Maybe we could help each other," and gave me an appraising look. Though the remark seemed offhand, I figured this was her goal all along.

"If I can sell the idea to my superiors, would you be willing to work with us in exchange for an exclusive, inside story about drug smuggling in Chesapeake Bay?"

"Why the hell not?" I agreed. "I always said I'd do anything for a story."

She sat in silence a while, then stood up, giving my shoulder a gentle squeeze. "I'll be in touch," she said on her way out.

* * * *

About two o'clock that afternoon, Whitey parked his car in front of my cottage. He looked almost as bad as I felt, and I smothered a smirk at the white smudges on the seat of his pants. He held up a brown business envelope as he walked to the front porch. "I know pulling a switch on you was way cold, but I got to know we can trust you. You down with that? But that shit in the bar last night, I had to teach you a lesson."

I opened the envelope and fanned a handful of hundred-dollar bills. I gave him a hard stare. "Don't ever play me again, asshole. I won't be nobody's bitch," I snarled.

"It's all good, yo. Get back with you soon," Whitey said as he drove away.

I put the finishing touches on the boat's repairs and headed into town for more paint. While I was at the hardware store, Denise called my cell phone. The excitement in her voice was unmistakable as she told me that HIDU had a tip from the DEA that a mothership they've been monitoring was headed up the coast from the Caribbean. "Get ready for a drug drop," she said.

Motherships can carry over a hundred tons of drugs and typically linger fifty to a hundred miles out in international waters. Small ships then ferry the drugs closer in where they rendezvous with go-fast boats that can outrun most Coast Guard cutters.

Denise met me at the Piney Point Market the next day to brief me on the plan.

She told me the DEA was pressuring area law-enforcement agencies to prove their drug interdiction efforts are worth the millions in taxpayer money they've gotten over the years. "They say if we don't make a major bust soon, our funding might get cut," she said. "Hell, federal money's the only thing that keeps cops on the streets in communities all along the bay."

With information from the DEA and about my earlier dry run for Whitey, Denise said the HIDU team planned to nab the smugglers as they moved the drugs up the bay to the floating duck blind. The Coast Guard would seal off the bay along the Maryland-Virginia boundary after the smugglers' boat began its northward trek. A small flotilla of patrol boats would lie in ambush as the drug runners made their way to Taylor Cove. Crucial to the plan's success, all agreed, was that the best time to pounce would be while the drugs were being off-loaded onto the duck blind. The patrol boats would then close in, giving the smugglers no chance to get away.

After Denise left the market, I was putting groceries in my car when Whitey's shiny, clean convertible pulled up. "Time to go to work," he said and followed me home.

The drop was to be that night. Whitey's plan was for the *Lady J* to stand off, with no lights showing, to act as the smugglers' lookout. If anything went wrong, I was to warn them with four long blasts on my horn then make my getaway. If the drop went all right, though, I would pick up the drugs as before and head home. Whitey swore he'd be waiting at the dock behind my cottage.

Only this time a HIDU team would be there when he arrived.

As the *Lady J* took her lookout station that dark, drizzly night, I switched off her running lights, eased her engine into neutral, and waited. Denise in a dark green tactical uniform was out of sight in the tiny cabin, armed and ready. I pulled my knit cap tighter on my head and hunched deeper into my waterproof coat, ears straining for the sound of the speedboat's engines.

I heard Denise check her pistol. It felt strange having a woman carrying a .40-caliber Smith & Wesson scrunched up at waist level. I hoped her gun was pointing up and well to the side.

After what seemed like hours, the night air vibrated as the smugglers' powerful craft approached, its low, black silhouette barely visible in the gloom. I gave the pre-arranged all-clear signal of two long flashes from a red-lensed lantern. Their answer came a few seconds later. The boat continued past our position in a slow, wide turn, its wake slapping against the *Lady J*'s sides. I figured they were making their own security sweep and held my breath, hoping they wouldn't spot the ambush.

Apparently satisfied they were in the clear, the smugglers headed back toward us. Fifteen minutes at most, I thought, and the authorities would have the drug runners and their poisonous cargo in custody, and I could go back to being...what?

I barely had time to ponder my uncertain future when a blinding light swept over my boat. The smugglers were taking a closer look, and Denise made herself even smaller at my side. I shielded my eyes against the glare and gave a half-hearted wave in response to the unwelcome scrutiny. As the sleek craft circled, a shark eying its next meal, I prayed that denizen of darkness would soon be on its way to the drop point.

Before I could say amen, though, the entire area erupted in a cacophony of light and noise: the wail of police-boat sirens mixed with an amplified voice ordering the smugglers to heave to and drop their weapons. High-wattage search beams crisscrossed the misty darkness, and the flashing patrol lights gave the scene a nightmarish quality. Someone on the ambush team had jumped the gun, and Denise and I were caught in a dangeous crossfire as the smugglers tried to shoot it out in a high-speed getaway. It was just what their muscle boat was designed for.

A burst of machine gun fire splintered wood all around me. "Down!" Denise yelled and sprang at me. We tumbled to the deck, and she rolled into position to return fire. She got off three or four shots then dove for cover, unleashing a stream of curses as the smugglers swung around, dousing us with their wake.

Neither Denise nor I dared rise up to see what was going on, but we heard and felt enough to understand a little of what it must have been like for the allied forces hitting the beach at Normandy on D-Day. The *Lady J* rolled and wallowed in the water churned up by the police in pursuit of the smugglers high-tailing it south.

With the running gun battle receding into the distance, I risked a peek over the gunwales. Cold and wet from the rain and spray, I slumped down against the side, shaking. Denise, probably because her hand still gripped a loaded weapon, rose up with more courage to survey our surroundings. She gave a sharp yelp and dived back down as a glaring cone of light stabbed across my boat. Back to holding my breath and praying, I shuddered, huddling Denise to reassure her— and myself.

I started breathing again when a voice called, "Ahoy, the dead-rise. Are you all right?"

I left it up to Denise to answer the hail. My vocal cords refused to work.

The patrol craft came alongside the *Lady J*, and I pulled it close with my boathook, passing a line to a deckhand. "Lieutenant Cliff Thompson," an officer said, stepping aboard. "Is anyone injured?"

I accompanied the lieutenant to the cabin and turned on the work lights. Denise's left leg was bleeding, and a thick splinter protruded from the wound. I saw, too, that her jacket had two ragged holes in the back, the armored vest showing through.

"This job is murder on my clothing budget," Denise hissed through clenched teeth as an EMT with a bright yellow aid box scrambled aboard to tend to her injuries.

Just then, an insistent radio operator yelled for the lieutenant. An urgent message from the chase boat. The smugglers had eluded their pursuers and were headed back north. Thompson ordered Denise and me to board his forty-foot Boston Whaler, which was armed and considerably faster than the *Lady J*.

I switched off the engine and work lights on my battered, aging craft and took the Thermos of bourbon-laced coffee I'd prepared earlier from my cabin. Something to ward off the chill and steady the nerves.

As Denise boarded the patrol boat, I heard the speedboat's rumbling engines in the distance, followed by what looked and sounded like giant, demonic lighting bugs hurtling toward us.

The smugglers traveling at breakneck speed were rounding a spit of land at the entrance to Taylor Cove. They must have seen the patrol boat because they veered to port, trying to pass it on the side away from shore.

With one foot on the patrol boat, I hesitated a moment then passed the coffee to Denise and stepped back onto the *Lady J*. After all, I had made a promise to her namesake.

The reliable little engine caught with the first turn of my key. I spun the wheel, throttling to full power, and switched on all the lights. I made a quick mental calculation and set a course. Bearing down on the smugglers' boat, I hoped to force it back toward shore. Instead, the *Lady J* and I were in a deadly game of chicken. One of the thugs opened fire with a machine gun that ripped up still more chunks of her wood. Reluctantly, I figured the safest place for me would be in the water. So I set the wheel and bolted toward the stern. My escape was anything but graceful, and I swallowed a lot of water coming up for air in time to watch the *Lady J* close in fast on her target.

In their panic to avoid a head-on collision, the drug runners swung hard to starboard and ran aground in the rock-strewn shallows. The impact shredded the boat's fiberglass hull. Its powerful engines revved, and the twin propellers chewed the silt, gravel, and debris into a roiling slurry that splattered everywhere.

Sputtering and coughing, I was pulled from the water onto another police boat. With sadness, I watched the *Lady J* recede into the darkness.

As the patrol boat approached shore, I saw one of the smugglers had been thrown clear of the wreck. The other was slumped over the steering wheel. It was to have been a busy night for them, judging from the four duffle bags and several red, plastic fuel containers I saw in the speedboat's cockpit.

Wrapped in blankets a few minutes later, I shivered in the command boat's cabin as the smugglers in handcuffs were brought on board. I saw blood trickling down the driver's shiny head and across his face. The man who had been thrown from the boat had been bald, too. My heart pounded, and anger swelled as I recognized the hoodlums who had dumped me in the bay. Perhaps sensing my rising fury, Denise grabbed my arm, pulling me close. "Shelby, I don't know about you, but I sure could use a cup of your special coffee."

* * * *

My editor and the rest of the *Inside Access* staff gave me a warm welcome as I walked into the office. In twos and threes, they drifted over to ask what had happened and where I'd been during my sabbatical.

That afternoon I began writing my insider's account of drug smuggling in the Chesapeake Bay, untangling the spider's web of motherships, speedboats, stash houses, wholesalers, and street dealers. I worked like a fiend for three weeks, with my editor breathing down my neck and refilling my coffee cup so we could make the next deadline.

Soon every major news outlet in the country ran stories about my exposé and how it helped the DEA and the Coast Guard shut down the Compioso cartel's entire East Coast drug network. There was even some buzz about a potential Pulitzer Prize. While I was flattered by all that attention, the bottom line was that I had finally settled the score, saving lots of young lives, like Janette's.

I was working on another story when I signed for a FedEx delivery. In the package was a framed photograph of Denise and her uncle beside the *Lady J*, all patched up and freshly painted. A handwritten note read, "As long as their memory endures, the dead rise up within the hearts of the living. Anytime you need help with a story, you know where to find us."

I put the picture on my desk and resumed tapping away at my computer.

David Autry is a recovering newspaper reporter currently employed as a writer/editor for a national non-profit organization. Born in Memphis, Tennessee, his love of reading and writing sprang from the region's rich traditions of oral storytelling, music, and literature. He grew up reading hard-boiled detective stories, mysteries, spy thrillers, and many of the Beat writers, as well as the usual classics. That exposure to a broad array of styles and subjects helped solidify his preferences for what he likes to read and write. He lives in Olney, Maryland, with his wife and two cats.

THE FACTORY
by Harriette Sackler

Stacey Levine sat at her grandmother's dining room table. She'd just devoured a large bowl of cabbage soup along with three substantial pieces of *challah* and already her stomach was rebelling against so much food. She didn't know how she would tackle the brisket with fixings that was yet to come, not to mention the freshly baked apple pie. Nana Rebecca always prepared enough food for an army, and Stacey couldn't deny her the pleasure of seeing her granddaughter eat.

"So, darling. How was school this week?" Rebecca asked as she came into the dining room with more food.

"Pretty good. I took two exams and think I did well. Got an A on my creative writing project. And let me tell you about the paper I'm doing for my History of the U.S. Labor Movement class. I've chosen to focus on early twentieth-century New York City and the sweatshops in particular. It's hard to believe people actually worked under such horrible conditions back then, and in some places, still do. I swear, I don't think I could've survived."

After hearing her granddaughter's words, Rebecca stared into space for a moment, then turned to Stacey.

"My sweet girl, I'd like to tell you a story. I think it will be helpful to you as you write your paper. I ask only that you let me talk until I'm through and then you can ask me any questions you want."

"Of course, Nana."

"This is the story of my aunt Rivka."

* * * *

The large dim room was sweltering. No breeze penetrated the two filth-encrusted windows that faced the narrow airshaft separating the building from its neighbor. The whir and clack of forty sewing machines created an incessant noise that caused dull aches behind eyes. Lint and cotton dust floated through the air, clogging nostrils and causing a cacophony of sneezes, coughs, and hacking throughout the workday. There was little talk, because the women who worked here twelve hours a day simply didn't have the energy. It wasn't unusual for a worker to put her head down on her machine and succumb to the heat. Chances were she wouldn't be back the following day.

Rivka felt old. At the tender age of seventeen, she'd had little opportunity to experience the joys of youth. She barely remembered her life in the old country and wasn't sure at all that America was truly a land of freedom and opportunity. Unless opportunity meant the honor of spending half her life in this infernal hell. But on the Sabbath she spent a joyous day praying, eating, and resting with her beloved family. And dreaming. Of a life she'd never known.

Her father worked as a peddler. He pushed his cart through the teeming streets of the Lower East Side, selling used clothing to the poor. Her mother did piecework from home, embroidering *yarmulkes* and *taleisim* with fine artistry fit for kings. Her brother, Schmuel, sold newspapers, and Sarah, the baby, was spared the necessity, at least for several more years, of contributing to the family's support. The Lipskys were lucky. Their children could stay in school longer than most children on the Lower East Side because their father earned a bit more than others who lived in the tenements. But their dream of sending Schmuel to City College required all the family members to do their part.

* * * *

Elias Pearlstein was a lucky man. Thanks to his cousin, Reuben, he enjoyed a nice living as foreman of Mendelsohn's Menswear without having to actually labor as his workers did. He supervised. Or, more specifically, terrorized the women and girls in his charge. He pushed them beyond limits, finishing one more pair of pants by hand when their fingers could no longer guide the fabric through the sewing machine. He lengthened the workday and shortened the lunch break. He increased quotas and decreased pay. Nothing dramatic to cause a stir, but just enough to prove to Cousin Reuben that the factory was in good hands.

Best of all, Elias had a captive audience for his amorous advances. His wife had died in childbirth years before, and he now relied on the factory ladies to satisfy his sexual needs. The fact that they surrendered only under duress didn't bother Elias a bit.

"Good morning, Miss Stern. So nice to see you so bright and early. I know how much your wages mean to you. So no doubt you'll be most agreeable to a little meeting in my office after the workday."

"I beg you, Mr. Pearlstein, not to shame me. I work so hard, sewing all day. Isn't that enough?"

"Now, Miss Stern. You should be honored that you've caught my eye. You might find a little extra in your wages this week to help feed that family of yours. And, I assure you, no one will ever be the wiser."

Elias Pearlstein never once considered his behavior shameful.

* * * *

At seven o'clock on a Thursday evening, the girls rose from their machines and prepared to leave the factory. As Rivka stood and stretched to release the cramps in her back and legs, Monya Schwartz, a pretty young friend and neighbor, came over and whispered in Rivka's ear.

"Do you think we can walk home, just the two of us? I need to talk to you, and I don't want any of the others to hear."

"Of course we can. I hope everything is good in your house?"

Monya's eyes looked troubled and terribly sad. "We'll talk outside, Rivka," she said.

As a parade of tired young women made its way toward the narrow stairway of the five-story building, they were forced to pass Mr. Pearlstein's office. Rivka was surprised and relieved that today, unlike most days, he was not standing at his door, smirking at them in his usual wolfish manner. Then from behind his closed door came an angry bellow. "You're a *gonif*! I'm done with you, you thief. Get out, and don't let me set eyes on you again!" Another poor soul, protesting a cut in already meager wages, would be without a job tomorrow, Rivka thought as she hurried down the stairs.

When they reached the street, Rivka and Monya linked arms and slowly headed toward home. This was the one time of day when they could enjoy a moment of leisure before family chores in their crowded apartments would occupy them for the rest of the evening.

"Monya, it seems the weight of the world is on your shoulders today. Tell me what's troubling you. Maybe I can help."

Monya's lips quivered, and tears filled her eyes.

Rivka felt alarm growing. "Tell me," she urged.

Monya hesitated. "Rivka, I know that I'm a mouse, a creature afraid of her own shadow," she said in a quiet, halting voice. "It would be unthinkable for me to raise a fuss about anything."

Rivka disagreed. "Monya, you're a gem. A perfect daughter. A good friend. Why is this not a good thing?"

"Because I can't defend myself! I let bad things happen. I can't stand up to anybody."

Rivka was confused. "Tell me. What's happened to make you so critical of yourself?"

Monya wavered. There were certain things that one just didn't share. It was forbidden. Shameful. Not done. But Rivka was her closest friend, and Monya felt torn apart. She needed to talk about it.

"I'll tell you. You'll surely think ill of me afterward, but I'll have to take that chance. You see, Pearlstein, that *momzer*, you should pardon my language, knows which of the girls at the factory are just like me. The obedient ones who do what they're told. He tries to take advantage of us. Touch us. When we protest, he threatens us and reduces our wages. I'm worn out, Rivka. For all my work at the factory, I bring home less money each week."

"Monya, why haven't you told me about this before?"

"Oh, Rivka, I didn't think you'd understand. You're so strong, so unlike me. You'd never find yourself in this kind of situation. And, you know, we don't talk about such things. Shame is a burden we carry alone."

Rivka felt her blood boil at the thought of what Monya had endured. Well, no more.

* * * *

The following morning, Rivka rose earlier than she normally did and hurried to Mendelsohn's. Employees started work at seven a.m., but Pearlstein and the shipping department started their day at six. Rivka knew the factory would be quiet and the upper floors deserted, except for Pearlstein's unpleasant presence. When she arrived, she quietly made her way up the stairs to the fifth floor. When she reached Pearlstein's office, she stood in front of the door, taking deep breaths to ease the tightness in her chest and the uncontrollable trembling of her hands. Several moments later, resolved to do what was necessary, she softly knocked on the door. No answer. Had Pearlstein not come to the factory at his usual time? Rivka knocked again, louder this time, calling out his name.

"Go away!" a slurred, hoarse voice responded.

"Mr. Pearlstein, it's Rivka Lipsky. I need to talk to you about a very important matter. May I come in?"

"Ah, Miss Lipsky, have you come to offer Pearlstein comfort in his time of need? Come in. Come in. I would welcome the company of such a lovely young lady."

Rivka steeled herself and opened the door. The malignant stench from the office made her gasp. The putrid odors of an unwashed body, liquor, and vomit were enough to make her want to turn and flee.

"Mr. Pearlstein," she managed to say, fighting the nausea that threatened to erupt. "I've learned how you take advantage of your position of authority, harassing girls at the factory in a most unacceptable manner and then reducing their wages to punish them for not complying with your demands. This must stop immediately."

Even in his inebriated state, Pearlstein looked incredulous.

"Rivka, Rivka, you're admonishing me for my behavior? Do you forget to whom you're talking? Since when does a woman, no a girl, have the *chutzpah* to speak in that manner to her boss? It's unheard of."

Rivka's anger erupted. To think that this pig, this *chazer,* felt he was better than her. She took a breath and forced herself to speak calmly.

"Mr. Pearlstein, there are important people working to make life better for factory workers. They invite news of the workplaces they call 'sweatshops.' I intend to tell as many of them as I possibly can about you. How long do you think your esteemed cousin will keep you in his employ when he becomes a target of those who are friends of the working poor?"

Without warning, Pearlstein roared and rose clumsily to his feet. In a second, he rounded his desk and grabbed at Rivka. Shaking off his hands, she turned and ran to the office door. But even in his diminished state, Pearlstein got his arms around her as she entered the hall. Horrified that she had not considered the prospect of putting herself in danger by coming here at this hour, Rivka gathered all her strength and pushed Pearlstein. He teetered in the small stairwell for a few seconds before falling backward. In an instant, with crashing glass and a frightened cry, he fell through the large window over-looking the airshaft.

Rivka stood stunned. It took a moment for her mind to register what had just happened. She stuffed her fist into her mouth to stifle the scream that rose inside her. She wanted to run away, but even as shock numbed her mind and body, she forced herself to think. She slowly moved toward the shattered window and carefully leaned through to look down into the airshaft. At the bottom, five floors below, Pearlstein lay sprawled amid the garbage and debris. Blood drained from his nose and mouth.

A few moments passed before Rivka knew what she had to do. She turned toward the stairs, opened her mouth, and screamed. "Help! Oh, my God. Somebody help!"

In no time, Rivka heard the sound of tramping feet making their way toward her with shouts of "what's wrong" and "we're coming" echoing in the stairwells. Soon John Gerotti and Isaac Levy, two of the workmen who always arrived at the factory early to pack finished garments into shipping crates, reached her, gulping to push air into their strained lungs.

"Are you all right, miss?" Mr. Gerotti asked Rivka in a concerned voice. "Are you hurt?"

"No, no, I'm fine. But something terrible has happened to Mr. Pearlstein. He's lying in the airshaft. When I came upstairs to finish some work left from yesterday, I saw the broken window. I looked out and discovered him crumpled and bleeding outside. Please, help him."

Mr. Levy ran to the broken window and gazed down. "I think it's too late for him. He has the look of the dead. But I'll go down anyway to be sure. Johnny, could you call a doctor and the police? Take Miss Lipsky with you. She doesn't look so good."

* * * *

The investigation into the death of Elias Pearlstein lasted only two days. Not one person interviewed by the police had anything good to say about the man. Interestingly, his cousin and employer revealed that the evening before, he had fired Pearlstein for stealing funds from the business. If Rivka had known this, she never would have made her morning visit to him. The problems at the factory would have been resolved with his departure. The raised voices she had heard the previous evening were the voices of the cousins.

No one questioned Rivka's account of Pearlstein's death. On the contrary, she received comfort from her co-workers and more sympathetic treatment by the police than she had expected. After all, in the old country the police were to be feared and avoided at all costs. Reuben Mendelsohn hired a new foreman who treated the workers better. Life improved at the factory, but the tragic episode was not over for Rivka. It haunted her. She could not eat or sleep well. Her fellow workers whispered amongst themselves about her drawn and pale appearance. Her mother, alarmed at Rivka's painful thinness, attempted to entice her with thick soups and warm breads. Rivka never smiled and always seemed preoccupied. Every time she entered Mendelsohn's, she relived the horror of Pearlstein's death and wondered if her inability to put the past behind her was a reflection of God's displeasure with her deceit.

* * * *

On a cold and blustery December morning, Rivka and Monya made their way through the crowded streets to the factory.

"So tell me," Monya said, "which of the world's problems are you attempting to solve this morning?"

Rivka stopped walking, faced Monya, and with a sad expression spoke. "I do have some news for you, and I pray that you'll understand. You know, I haven't been myself since the day of Pearlstein's death. I haven't been able to put it behind me, and every day I relive those moments. I truly believe that it would be best for me to leave Mendelsohn's and move on to a new job. I've been looking for other work and have found a place where I can sew better fabrics and get a higher wage. It's a bit farther uptown near a park and a university, would you believe. This factory is in a large building with elevators. Such luxury!"

"That's wonderful, Rivka. I shall miss seeing you every day, but we'll see each other on the Sabbath and have so much news to share each week."

"Yes," Rivka said. "This will be a good change for me."

* * * *

Rebecca grew silent.

"Nana, what a touching story. But how do you know the details? You told me your aunt Rivka died before you were born."

"That's true, Stacey. But my aunt kept a journal that was found among her belongings. Years ago, my mother passed it on to me. I've always felt it was far too personal to share, but I think it's good for you to know this piece of your family's history."

Stacey was touched by her grandmother's trust and had one more question to ask.

"Nana, how did Rivka die? Was she ill?"

"Ah. I didn't quite finish the story, darling. The name of Rivka's new employer was the Triangle Waist Company."

Stacey's eyes widened. "No! I've read a lot about that place. It was notorious. The Triangle Waist fire was one of the worst the city had seen. Over a hundred people, mostly young women, died there that day."

"Actually, 146, to be exact. Including my aunt," Rebecca said, wiping tears from her eyes. "The new place of employment Rivka thought would be so much better was just another sweatshop. So much for luxury!"

Harriette Sackler is a longtime member of the Malice Domestic Board of Directors and serves as grants chair. She is a past Agatha Award nominee for "Mother Love," her story that appeared in *Chesapeake Crimes II.* Harriette's writing background includes public relations and nonprofit fundraising materials. An avid pet lover, she is vice president of House with a Heart Senior Pet Sanctuary. Harriette lives in the D.C. suburbs with her husband, Bob, and their five pups. She has two married daughters and makes a point of thoroughly spoiling her two grandbabies, Ethan and Makayla.

THE LORD IS MY SHAMUS
by Barb Goffman

You'd think after all these years, I wouldn't be nervous in his presence. Yet my sandals shook as I approached the swirling cloud.

"You asked to see me?" I crooked my head, trying—but failing—to spot him through the mist. Why was he always such an enigma?

"Yes." His booming voice echoed. "I'm sending you back to Earth to do some investigating for me."

"Investigating?"

"A man has died, and I'd like you to probe those who knew him best. Find out what happened."

Now I know better than anyone that it's not my place to question God. He has his reasons for what he does. But come on. He's omniscient. Why would he need me to investigate anything for him?

"Umm...okay," I said. "But don't you already know what happened?"

He chuckled. "Well, yes, I do. But you of all people understand suffering and the need to know why it happens. So I want you to help this man's family by looking into his death and encouraging the killer to admit his sins and repent."

"The killer? You mean—"

"Yes. This, Job, is murder."

* * * *

In a blinding flash of light, I found myself in a city. Based on the accents, I figured it was Manhattan—though it could've been Miami or Fort Lauderdale or, really, anywhere in South Florida. I took a moment to take in the sights. Tall buildings. Automobiles zipping by. And the women walking around immodestly in a state of undress. Bare arms and legs and, in a few cases, midriffs. I knew how the Earth had changed during my years in the afterworld—I like keeping up on things—but actually seeing it in person? *Oy vey!*

I glanced down and noticed that my apparel had changed, too. Now I was wearing modern clothes: khaki pants and a pale blue polo shirt. I combed my fingers through my hair. Shorn! My long flowing locks were gone. Cropped to my ears. I raked my fingers over my face and breathed a deep sigh of relief. I'd been allowed to keep my beard, though it apparently had been trimmed and combed. I know I shouldn't care about my appearance, but after you've had the same look as many centuries as I have, you get kind of attached to it.

I turned left from the street corner. The avenue had been busy, but this side street was quieter. Trees and brownstones. A good place to think. My mind drifted back to God. He'd apparently changed my appearance so I'd fit in. And he'd dropped me in the victim's neighborhood, I gathered, so I could get started straight away. But he couldn't be bothered to tell me the killer's name so I could quickly get him to confess and repent? *That* I had to figure out on my own?

I rolled my eyes. (Yes, I'd atone for that later.) Thousands of years had passed, but the Lord still liked to play his little games. I guess when you're all-knowing, yanking my chain helps keep things interesting.

I stepped off the sidewalk, leaned against a nice shady tree, and took a few moments to try to think things through. I had no idea where to go. I patted my pockets. No money. Nowhere to spend the night. I didn't even know the victim's name. *Hey, Lord, how 'bout a little help down here?*

Frustrated, I slapped my hands against my thighs and heard something crinkle. That right pocket had been empty just a moment ago. I reached in and pulled out two scraps of paper. The first one was an obituary for Bruce Goldenblatt, a real-estate investor who had died the previous Saturday, leaving behind a wife and three daughters. The second scrap had an address printed on it—for the brownstone right in front of me.

I glanced up. *Nice aim. And thanks for the assist.*

Time to get down to business. I gazed at the house. Sparkling windows. Spotless front steps bookended by gleaming black wrought-iron railings. Beside the left railing, a handicapped ramp ran from the sidewalk to the stoop. This family might have faced tragedy before. I hoped I could help them now, at least.

It was after the funeral so the family would be sitting *shiva* for seven days, mourning their loved one and focusing on their loss. Who was I to intrude on their grief? While it would be a great *mitzvah* to make a *shiva* call, visitors should be friends and family. I wasn't either. But they'd all be there. An opportunity too good to miss.

I tilted my head, thinking. I could pretend to be an old friend (real old) of Goldenblatt, but they might ask me questions about him that I couldn't answer. I tapped my index finger against my lips. Ah. I'd be a grief counselor, sent over by the rabbi. That should work.

I made my way up the front steps and rang the bell. As I waited, I heard muffled yelling from inside. Soon a girl, maybe fourteen years old with long dark hair, yanked back the door. She was barefoot, wearing a short denim skirt and a low-cut, white tank top, and chewing something pink. Gum, I guessed, though I hadn't seen it firsthand before. Her toenails and fingernails were pink, too. I never would have allowed my daughters to dress that way.

"Hi?" she said. It was a statement, but it came out like a question.

"I don't care!" someone shrieked from behind her. "I don't want children at my wedding."

"How do you expect me not to invite your cousins after they just came to the funeral?" another woman screeched back. "It would be a *shanda*!"

"Too bad!" the first voice screamed. "It's My! Special! Day!"

What was I walking into? "I'm sorry to intrude," I told the girl. "My name is Jo...Joseph." *Close call.* "I'm a grief counselor. Your rabbi suggested I stop by."

The girl turned her head. "Mom! There's some grief counselor here!"

So much yelling. Maybe the family was hard of hearing.

As the girl backed away, a round, middle-aged woman approached the door. Did hair that blond come naturally? She smiled. "Yes?"

"Mrs. Goldenblatt?" She nodded. "Your rabbi sent me over. He thought I might be able to help you during this difficult time."

I extended a hand. "I'm Joseph…Bookman. Grief counselor. I'm so sorry for your loss."

"Rabbi Cohen sent you? Well, please come in."

I walked into a small entryway with a glass table in the middle. A large ceramic bowl filled with apples and pears sat on top. To my left was a staircase, straight ahead ran a long hallway with some closed doors lining the left wall, and a large living room was on my right. It had white leather couches, oriental rugs, and glass tables that matched the one in the entryway.

I blinked a couple times, confused. I saw no low stools for mourners to sit on. The mirror on the living-room wall remained uncovered. The woman wasn't even wearing a torn black ribbon in memory of her husband. Except for the fruit bowl in the entryway, which could have been a condolence gift, I saw nothing I'd expect in a home sitting *shiva*. Was I at the correct address?

"It's very nice that Rabbi Cohen has been thinking of us, but really, we're doing just fine," Mrs. Goldenblatt said, motioning me to follow her.

She led me through the house into a shiny chrome kitchen. *Now this was more like it!* Baskets and trays of food covered nearly every available counter, no doubt condolence gifts from friends and family.

The girl who had answered the door trailed behind us, then picked up a mewing gray kitten and climbed onto a bar stool. An older girl sat at a round table staring at a computer screen. An even older girl—a young woman, really—sat at the same table with piles of papers and magazines spread out in front of her. All three girls had the same thin nose, brown eyes, and long dark hair. None of them wore a black ribbon either.

"Girls, this is Mr. Bookman," the mother said. "He's a grief counselor. The rabbi sent him over."

They all looked at me like I'd sprouted another head. I glanced at my shoulders. Nope. No extra head. Thank goodness. That would have been hard to explain, though I'm sure *someone* would have thought it was a riot.

Where to begin? "Again, I'm so sorry for your loss, Mrs. Goldenblatt. And you girls."

"Where are my manners?" the mother said. "Please call me Marjorie. And these are my daughters, Anne, Kayla, and Lauren."

"Stop calling me Kayla," the middle girl said with gritted teeth. "Kay. My name is Kay."

"I'm so sorry, *Kay.*" Marjorie threw her hands in the air. "I did have a role in naming you, you know. Seventeen years you've been Kayla, but noooo. Now suddenly you're Kay."

Oh, yes. A big happy family.

"Kay," I said. "This must be a very hard time for you."

She shrugged. "Yeah. Dad was supposed to take me to look at colleges—I'll start college next fall—but now I have to wait till Mom has time to go. And who knows when that's gonna be. She's completely wrapped up in planning Anne's wedding."

"Lord give me strength," Marjorie said. "I told you I'd find time to take you."

"When?" Kay screeched.

"Soon!" Marjorie yelled back.

This is how they behave with company?

"A wedding," I said to the oldest girl. "How wonderful."

"Yeah, you'd think so," Anne said. "Until your mother starts foisting relatives on you that you don't want to invite." She looked at me with a hopeful smile. "I think the bride should get to choose her own guests, even if she's not paying for the reception. Don't you?"

Oh boy. I didn't want to get into the middle of this. "Well, are they relatives on your father's side of the family? It might be nice to include them, considering his recent passing."

Anne's eyes narrowed, obviously displeased. "Daddy wouldn't have wanted them invited either. He thought our plans were way too expensive. He kept wanting to cut everything down, including the guest list."

"Well, we don't have that problem now, do we?" Marjorie said, striding toward Anne. "Thanks to the life insurance, you can have the big fancy wedding you want. I don't think it's asking very much to invite your cousins! And you!" She turned to Kay. "Stop moping. At least now you can go to any college you want."

She took a deep breath and faced me. "I'm sorry. It's rude of us to talk about money in front of a virtual stranger. It's just been so stressful. Before Bruce died, we'd been having money problems. With the downturn in the economy, Kayla—Kay—was going to have to attend a *state* school, and my Anne would have to have a *scaled-down* wedding. Now Bruce is gone, and so are our money problems. It doesn't seem right."

Indeed. Not right at all. All three of these ladies had a reason to kill.

"What happened to your husband, if I might ask? He was so young," I said.

"He tripped. Fell down the stairs," said a raspy voice behind me. "Broke his neck."

I turned to see an old man with heavy wrinkles around his nose and eyes wheeling himself into the room. He had white hair like mine and a long white beard dotted with crumbs.

I glanced up for a moment. *How come my beard had to be trimmed so much if this guy can wear his beard long?* No response. Figures.

"Dad," Marjorie said. "I'd like you to meet Joseph Bookman. He's a grief counselor. Rabbi Cohen sent him."

"Nice to meet you. I'm Saul," he said as we shook hands. His accent sounded Eastern European. "Terrible thing that's happened. Just terrible."

"Dad witnessed the accident," Marjorie said. "None of the rest of us were home," she added quickly. A bit too quickly, if you ask me.

"What did Mr. Goldenblatt trip on?" I asked Saul.

"My kitten," Lauren, the youngest girl, said, her gaze glued to the feline in her arms. "Squeaker didn't mean to do it!"

"I'm sure she didn't," I said. Especially since I didn't buy the story for a minute.

"Come," Saul said, as he grabbed a pretzel from a bowl on the counter. "I'll show you where it happened."

He wheeled himself toward the front of the house, munching, the wooden floor creaking underneath. "I'm sure the rabbi meant well in sending you over," he said when we were out of earshot of the kitchen. "But I think it's best if the girls don't dwell on this."

He stopped by the front door, clearly wanting me to leave. But I had a job to do.

I turned to the long staircase. "Is this where Mr. Goldenblatt fell?"

"Yeah." Saul rolled up beside me. "The kitten came out of nowhere. Bruce was on his way up, tripped, and fell to the bottom. Poor Lauren's been blaming herself. I really wish she wouldn't."

"It's her cat?" I asked.

"Yep." He nodded. "For good now."

"What do you mean?"

"Lauren only got the kitten a couple months ago. Bruce was terribly allergic. He wanted her to take it back to the pound, but Lauren's attached to Squeaker. She desperately wanted to keep her. Marjorie told Bruce he should keep trying the allergy shots, though to be fair they weren't working." He shrugged. "So now the girl has no father, but she has a cat. Not the best trade off, if you ask me."

Me either. Now all the women in the house had a motive. The yelling in the kitchen resumed, something about chicken or fish. At least they weren't considering pork.

"That must have been a horrible thing to see," I said.

Saul stared at the floor. "Yeah, it was terrible."

Was the old man covering for someone? One of them could have pushed Bruce down the stairs. Did the mother care more about throwing a fancy wedding and sending her daughter to an expensive college than she did about her husband? Or was the bride so selfish that she'd kill her father for the life insurance money? Or her sister with the nickname—was attending some impressive school that important to her? Or the youngest one? Did she choose a kitten over her father?

Sheesh. I'd like to believe none of them was capable of such a horror. Unfortunately I feared otherwise.

"You live here?" I asked Saul.

"Yeah, ever since my Estelle died five years ago." He nodded at a room off the hallway. "Moved in there. It used to be Bruce's home office, but he was nice enough to convert it into a bedroom for me." He rolled closer. "Look, Mr. Bookman, I want you to know, these girls loved their father. And Marjorie loved her husband. I know how it must have sounded back there. So much bickering, especially at a time like this. But that's just their way."

I bent down so Saul and I would be eye to eye, and I laid a hand on his arm. "It must be hard for you, being the only man in the house. Now that Bruce is gone, you're their protector."

He nodded. "Not that I'm really needed. Marjorie's a very strong woman."

"Do you go to *shul*, Saul?" I asked, rising.

"Synagogue? Of course, on the High Holy Days. It's not so easy getting around with this chair, but I manage. We'll all go together next week for *Rosh Hashanah*."

"A time to ask for forgiveness of sins." I began pacing. "There are many sins in this world. It can often seem confusing. If you're trying to help someone you love—to protect them from the consequences of something they've done—is that a sin?"

Saul sat quietly for a moment. "I'd like to think that when God closes the Book of Life each *Yom Kippur*, that he considers everything a person has lived through and everything he's done, not just one act. We all know good men can do bad things."

"And good women."

He stared at me, his lips curling. He wanted to tell me what happened. I could see it.

"Mr. Bookman," he finally said. "I think you should go."

"Go? Already?" Marjorie approached us with a plate of *rugelach*. "You just got here. And I haven't even offered you anything to eat or drink."

I wasn't getting anywhere with Saul. Maybe I could work on Marjorie directly. I turned to her, selected a piece of pastry filled with raisins, and smiled. "A glass of water would be nice. Thank you."

Saul wheeled to his bedroom, muttering to himself, while I followed Marjorie to the kitchen.

An hour later, my stomach was stuffed, my head was pounding from all the yelling, and I knew more about the impending wedding than anyone would ever want to know. (Apparently having the same vase and flowers at every table is out. Each table needs its own "pop of style," whatever that means.) But I wasn't any closer to figuring out which of these women needed to unburden herself, and I had the feeling I was wearing out my welcome. I needed to speak to each one alone. But how?

Just then the kitten scampered past. *Ah.* I glanced up. *Thanks.*

"Lauren," I said. "I can tell you feel bad about Squeaker tripping your dad. Why don't we take a little walk and talk about it?"

"Okay," she said and hopped off her barstool.

"I hear your dad was allergic to Squeaker," I said as we entered the hallway, heading toward the front of the house.

She shuffled next to me, focusing on the floor. "Yeah. Anytime Dad was in the same room with Squeaker, his eyes turned red and he started sneezing."

"Must have been hard for you."

"Uh huh." She looked up. "Dad wanted me to give Squeaker back, but Mom convinced him to keep taking the allergy shots. He told me he'd try them for another month, but if things didn't get any better..."

"How'd that make you feel?"

"Mad. I mean I know it wasn't Dad's fault, but why couldn't I have a pet like everyone else?"

I couldn't tell if she was just a typical self-involved teen or something worse. I needed to test her.

"You know," I said as we approached the front staircase, "your grandpa could only see what occurred from a distance. Maybe it just looked like your dad tripped on Squeaker. Maybe he actually tripped on something else. Loose carpeting, perhaps."

Her eyes lit up. "You think?"

She raced to the stairs and scrutinized each one. I followed her up. She looked so hopeful. She really believed it could be true. A good feeling rose in my heart. She couldn't have pushed her father.

When we reached the top, she turned to me, shoulders hunched. "I don't see any loose carpeting. Thanks for trying, Mr. Bookman. I guess Squeaker really is to blame." She burst into tears and ran down the hall. A moment later, a door slammed and loud music began blaring from behind the door.

Great. I made a child cry. More to repent for.

I bent down to examine the top step. Had God sent me on a wild-goose chase? Could Goldenblatt really have just fallen over the cat? Heck, maybe he threw himself down the stairs to get away from all this squabbling. I needed to talk to the other girls to—

I felt hands on my shoulder blades. Then a shove! I began tumbling down the stairs. *Oof! Urk! Hey, my suffering was supposed to be over!*

I landed at the bottom and smacked my brow hard against the entryway table's base. Apples and pears began falling on my head. *Lord, what have I done to deserve this?*

When the pounding stopped, I opened my eyes. Blinked. The room spun. I shut my eyes and waited for someone to come help me up, fearing it could take a while. Between the music upstairs and the yelling from the kitchen, I doubted anyone had heard me fall.

Hey. Wait a minute. Who pushed me?

Not Lauren. I would have seen her coming. Couldn't have been Marjorie. I could clearly hear her in the kitchen. And there was Anne, yelling back, also in the kitchen. And Kay's complaints were wafting down the hallway, too.

What the heck?

The floor creaked, and I felt a shadow fall over me. "God, forgive my terrible temper again," Saul said. "But he was trying to hurt my girls, to blame them for what happened."

Saul?

I opened my eyes. His flew wide.

"You're alive?" he said.

"*You* pushed me?" I said, eyeing his wheelchair. "And Bruce? But how?"

He suddenly appeared very old and scared. "The elevator." He nodded toward one of the closed doors in the hall. "Bruce had it installed for me when I moved in."

An elevator in a house? I guess I wasn't as up on the modern world as I'd thought.

"I don't understand," I said, trying to get up but slumping back down. *Oy*, my head hurt. "He let you move into his home. Gave you his office. Enabled you to get around the whole house, apparently. Why would you do this to him, Saul?"

He paused. For a moment he seemed far away, lost in thought. Then he held out his left forearm and pushed up the sleeve. Tattooed numbers. I sighed deeply.

"I was a teenager when we were sent to the camps," he said. "Auschwitz. I never saw my mother and sisters again." He shivered and shook his head, as if he could make the memories disappear. "I was the only member of my family to survive. When the war ended, I promised myself I'd create a new family and I'd protect them from everything."

"But Bruce loved you and the girls. Didn't he? How was he a threat?"

Saul gazed toward the kitchen, where the argument had moved on to the flavor of the wedding cake. "Marjorie and the girls raise their voices, but not Bruce. Never Bruce. Until the economy turned, and he lost a lot of money in the market." Saul wrung his hands. "He wanted Marjorie and the girls to sacrifice. A small wedding. A state school. That I could understand, but he had no right to yell at my Marjorie."

He paused. I stared quietly at him, hoping my silence would encourage him to continue. Finally, he did.

"The day Bruce died," Saul said, "he and Marjorie had another argument about money, much louder than the one going on right now. He called her extravagant, said she was spoiling the girls. Marjorie called him a tightwad and insisted on her way, but Bruce said that for once he was going to get his way. Marjorie's waterworks wouldn't work. Marjorie stormed out, and Bruce headed up the stairs here. I was at the top, where I'd been listening. I couldn't help myself. I was so angry. My Marjorie deserved to be treated like a queen! You don't scream at queens." Tears spilled from his eyes. "No one suspected a thing. Just like they won't with you."

He grabbed the ceramic fruit bowl and raised it over my head.

"Daddy, no!" Marjorie ran toward us. "Not again!"

Saul's arms quivered as he lowered the bowl. I let out a deep breath. I'd died once before. Believe me, once had been enough.

Marjorie grabbed the bowl from Saul's outstretched hands and clutched it to her chest.

"You know?" he asked her.

A tear ran down her cheek. "I thought you did it for the money, Daddy. So Anne could have her wedding and Kayla could go to a good school. I didn't know you killed Bruce because of me. You shouldn't have. I loved him. He was a good man."

Saul leaned back in the chair, his face ashen. "It was the yelling, Marjorie. I couldn't stand that he yelled at you."

"I'm a grown woman, Daddy. I could have handled it."

"I know," he said quietly. "I lost my temper. I'm sorry."

While they were talking, I'd struggled to my feet. My head hurt, but I'd felt worse. Marjorie seemed to notice me at that moment.

"Oh, Mr. Bookman. Please don't turn my father in. He did a terrible thing, but his heart was in the right place. He's suffered so much already, and we need him here with us."

I looked at her and then at Saul for a good while, and I understood why God had sent me.

"You should go to your rabbi, both of you. Confess what happened. He'll help you find your way."

Marjorie's eyes widened, afraid, but Saul nodded.

"You're right, Bookman. I'll go. We'll both go." He held out his hand, and I shook it. "It'll be good getting it all off my chest. Maybe we can find a way to let Lauren know that she wasn't to blame because of her cat. And I'm sorry about…this." He gestured at the bowl and had the decency to look sheepish.

I nodded and turned back to Marjorie. "I have to ask. You said you weren't home at the time. How did you know what happened?"

"Yeah," Saul said. "How?"

She set the bowl on the table. "I was only gone a couple minutes, Daddy. Remember? Got as far as the corner, then turned around. I came in, saw Bruce, and screamed. You called from upstairs that you were on the phone with 911. You said Bruce had tripped over Squeaker halfway up the stairs. Fell all the way down."

"So?" Saul asked.

"I knew Bruce couldn't have tripped over Squeaker. Bruce would have known if Squeaker were anywhere near him. He started sneezing whenever the cat came within five feet." She sniffed hard and reached out, plucking a large crumb from Saul's beard. "And then I saw some pretzel crumbs on Bruce. You're the only one of us who eats pretzels, Daddy. You eat them constantly, as if you're afraid we'll run out of food. I knew Bruce must have made it to the top of the stairs, and you must have touched him. It's the only way crumbs from your beard would have fallen onto him. So I knew you lied about how he fell."

Saul turned my way, looking surprised yet also proud. "That's my girl," he said. "A regular Columbo."

* * * *

I said my goodbyes, left the brownstone, and by the time I reached the sidewalk, *poof*! I was home again. My hair was long, and I had on my favorite robe and sandals.

The swirling cloud appeared before me. "A job well done, Job."

"So it was Saul, huh?" I said. "I didn't suspect him for a minute. I knew all about elevators, but I didn't know they put them in houses. That's what I get for taking classes from Moses. Sure, he knows his *Torah*, but he also got lost in the desert for forty years. I never should've expected he'd get all the details on the modern world right."

God chuckled.

"I hope I handled things the way you wanted," I said.

"Yes. You got Saul to confess his sin and Marjorie to admit she knew about it. Good work."

"Too bad I nearly had to die to do it," I said.

"Well," God said, "it's not like you haven't died before."

Easy for you to say.

"If there's nothing else," I said, "I think there's a pinochle game going on."

The mist began swirling more.

"I'll speak to you again soon, Job." If a cloud could wink, I'd swear this one did. "Hopefully things won't be so dangerous the next time."

Next time?!

Barb Goffman has been nominated four times for the Agatha Award for her short stories. In addition to writing short fiction, Barb has completed her first novel, *Call Girl*. She is program chair of the Malice Domestic mystery convention, is secretary of the Mid-Atlantic chapter of Mystery Writers of America, is a past president of the Chesapeake Chapter of Sisters in Crime, and has served as a coordinating editor of two *Chesapeake Crimes* anthologies, including this one. She lives in Virginia with her miracle dog, Scout, a three-time cancer survivor. Learn more at http://www.barbgoffman.com.

TO ADJUNCTS EVERYWHERE
by Ellen Herbert

I was sitting in my van in a dark corner of faculty parking, looking up at his windows—the only lit windows in Edgar Allen Poe Hall, home to George Henry University's English Department. The night was cold, and clear, and so far delightfully free of the usual roaming zombies.

"Tonight's the night," I whispered to the sole Nobel Laureate in Literature ever lured to GHU. Closing my eyes, I could see Kaplan Kossek, a Polish Jew exiled in this suburban Virginia gulag, sitting in his office. I imagined him composing his lyrical gory stories about life in Krakow the old-fashioned way, with fountain pen on vellum paper. Every so often he would glance out at the misty woods separating Poe Hall from the parking lot and know I was out here, waiting to shiver and thrill at his next book. I was his reader.

Not that he knew me, not personally. I wasn't so presumptuous. Still Kappy was a great writer with a huge heart and could perhaps sense me out here. I was a homeless adjunct professor living in my van ever since I received my master's of fine arts degree from GHU five years ago. I read Kappy's wondrous works by flashlight, existing on a diet of microwave Ramen Noodles, clothing myself from the campus Lost and Found.

Of course, as an English adjunct, I accepted that I was the lowest form of life at GHU. This state university's caste system was more severe than India's. My fate was to teach three composition courses a semester so the Tenured Ones could kill more trees publishing their books at academic presses, books no one cared about, books no one would ever read. Books the Tenured Ones hoped would propel them not to fame or fortune, but to the next rung on GHU's promotion ladder.

Not that I had a shot at fame or fortune. On the contrary, as an English adjunct, I was an anonymous cog in their education factory and had taken a vow of poverty as well. My GHU salary was so small I couldn't afford an apartment. On the bright side, I made enough to pay for my campus parking space and a membership to the university gym, where I could clean up and shower. Still I didn't look forward to another winter sleeping in my van. Yet I felt warm when I remembered I slept under Kaplan Kossek's windows, his golden lights burning into the dawn, his work ethic and dedication to his art inspiring me to perhaps write a lyrical horror story of my own some day.

And tonight I would meet him at last, because I had something important to say to him, something I hoped would give him peace of mind.

Opening the van's door, I stepped out and looked around campus, silent and deserted as usual. Acres of asphalt parking lots surrounded GHU, a commuter school, meaning everyone commuted the hell away as soon as classes ended. Neither students nor faculty could stand to be at GHU a moment longer than necessary. Maybe they sensed the campus was haunted. Yes, haunted, though only I and—perhaps Kappy—knew its haunting wasn't so bad. In fact, once the students and faculty left, GHU turned magical, almost unicorn-leaping magical.

Pine needles crunched underfoot as I walked to Poe Hall, careful not to step too close to the burial mounds. GHU's younger tenure-track faculty regularly killed tenured profs and buried them here. If they didn't, the geezers would soldier on into eternity, shuffling to class on walkers, wearing their Depends, Fixodent oozing from their clattering dentures, since their egos wouldn't allow them to retire. But the lazy junior faculty often buried them in graves too shallow. So shallow the oldies managed to claw their way up and out and go on to class, where they cut off their hearing aids and sawed on about Victorian vulgarities or postmodern feminist theory in literature of the Pacific Rim.

In *U.S. News & World Report's* annual college rankings, GHU was known for having the largest percentage of zombie faculty, especially in our famous Economics Department, in which they were almost the majority. Many of the undead regularly appeared on CNN or Fox News, where they un-ironically advised that we must cut Medicaid, Medicare, cut everything except the Defense Department's budget.

I started and whirled when I saw movement from the corner of my eye, but it was only Phoebe, my favorite ghost, emerging from the hillside's rainy mist like a vision.

"Madam, where are you sallying out to this evening?" she called to me. Closing her yellow silk parasol, she drew closer.

As usual I marveled at her beauty, especially since she'd died in 1861 soon after the Battle of Bull Run. Her dewy skin was the color of coffee, and she possessed a grace unknown to women of my century. If not for her slight transparency, hardly noticeable in tonight's dim light, you would never have guessed she was a ghost.

"That dress is stunning on you," I said. "Did George give it to you?"

Phoebe had been a thirteen-year-old slave when George Henry took her as his mistress. While the great patriot Patrick Henry was famous for saying, "Give me liberty or give me death!" his younger brother George, also a patriot if a self-interested one, was remembered for saying, "Give me free markets unfettered by tariffs or regulation!" Hence he was not only the university's namesake but also the capitalist saint of GHU's Econ Department, where they had a life-size statue of him.

"Kindly refrain from addressing Mr. Henry by his given name," Phoebe said and walked beside me, her petticoat rustling, her basket of herbs swinging from her wrist. The land on which GHU stood was once George Henry's plantation, so Phoebe knew all the flora and fauna here and often gave me potions for my colds and flu. I couldn't have survived winters in my van without her herbal medicine since the university provided no health insurance for adjuncts. If we fell ill in the hallways or classrooms, our bodies were tossed into Dumpsters and sent off to landfills in Lorton.

"I meant no disrespect, Phoebe. I assure you." I took her arm. The nineteenth century was an era of formality and manners. Phoebe would brook no criticism of George Henry, who had given her a better education than any of the students here, undergraduates or grads, were likely to receive—better than I'd gotten with my MFA. Upon his death Master Henry had freed her, so she remained grateful even though I pointed out to her that today he would have been classified as a pedophile.

Phoebe and I had met the night a zombie econ professor reached out of his grave and latched onto her ankle. Phoebe was attempting to turn herself into mist and get away when I hacked off the zombie's hand with the spine of my thick *Pelican Shakespeare.*

"I'm much obliged to you," Phoebe had said with a curtsey. I'd helped pry his cold dead fingers from around her ankle, and we'd been close friends ever since.

We reached Poe Hall, where Phoebe stopped me. "Nora dear, it's unseemly for a young lady to call on a gentleman."

We often sparred about the manners and mores of our respective centuries. "Maybe if you'd called on your Robert, you wouldn't have to haunt these woods for eternity searching for him," I said.

She sighed and glanced down at the frilly gloves on her hands. "Perhaps so." I knew she didn't like to talk about the afterlife or the man she had loved and lost when good ol' George Henry sold him down the river.

"Wish me luck," I told her and stepped toward the dark doorway.

"Forget about that old writer and come ride the big dumbwaiter with me."

She meant the elevator in Ayn Rand Hall, home of GHU's hotshot Econ Department. The odd ten-story building sat on the hump of a hill, where its big glass elevator was connected to the structure's only wing, one that went off to the right, the far right. In their lobby, beside George Henry's statue, was a solid gold plaque on which their motto was engraved: *Avaritia est bona.* "Greed is good," Phoebe had translated the first time we saw it.

Smoothing my jeans, I said, "I have to meet Kaplan Kossek tonight." I'd worked up my courage and had to go through with it. "I have something important to tell him."

She shook her head, opened her parasol, and vanished into the starless night. She could appear and disappear at will, an advantage the dead have over the rest of us.

I entered Poe Hall, a mere four stories tall, with nary a working elevator or grandiose motto in sight. English majors needed to be a hardy lot. My life could attest to this. I trudged up the stairs to the top floor.

Kappy always worked late at night. I knew he did this to avoid contact with GHU students. From old photos I'd seen of him in *Poets & Writers*, he was always surrounded by students at Warsaw University. In Europe, students actually read books and treated great writers like rock stars, following them around, wanting to discuss literature and life with them, hanging on their every word.

I came to Kappy tonight to apologize for the fact that this was not the case here in the United States. A recent campus survey showed that ninety-nine percent of GHU students thought Kaplan Kossek was a preparatory course for medieval history. Not that Kappy should be insulted by this—a similar percentage had never heard of William Shakespeare or that the Earth was round.

GHU students were extremely focused. They cared only about their grade-point averages. All of them had double majors in badgering and harassing. Like predators, they could smell adjunct faculty across campus. They made sure to sign up for courses we adjuncts taught, knowing we weren't paid well enough to fight off their badgering and harassing over grades. Perhaps it was just as well that Kappy wasn't expected to teach any classes, only give the occasional guest lecture or reading.

I pushed through the doors of the English Department, everything dark around me, except for the honeyed beam of light coming from Kappy's office.

Following his light, I went down a long hallway past the offices of the Tenured Ones. Even though they were seldom on campus, the Tenured Ones got rooms with windows, the only windows in Poe Hall. Classrooms were pushed to the building's dark interior, where plastic moveable curtains served as walls. While classrooms in Ayn Rand Hall were outfitted with individual computers and overhead projectors, the English Department made do with dusty blackboards and stubby bits of yellow chalk.

When I saw the name, Kaplan Kossek, on his door, my heart began to drum. I knocked softly. Through the door's frosted glass pane, I could sort of see him from the back sitting just as I had imagined, slumped at his desk, hard at work.

When he didn't answer, I knocked harder, my knocks mirroring the pounding in my chest. "Mr. Kossek," I called but still no answer.

Maybe he had fallen asleep. I paused, wondering if I ought to wake him. He was in his eighties and not in good health. During the year and a half he'd been at GHU, he was forced to cancel all his lectures and readings due to illness. And the publication date of this latest book had been postponed twice. No one seemed to care about his health or these cancelations, except for me.

What if he had gotten sick tonight? What if he needed CPR or to be taken to the hospital? I had to get in there and check on him. But when I tried the knob, the door was locked.

Rushing to the English Department's central office, I slipped behind the high counter where the clerks sat, a place lowly adjuncts were forbidden to go. But I knew their secrets. From a hidden place beneath the head flunky's desk, I took the master key and ran back to Kappy's door.

Unlocking it, I hurried in. "Mr. Kossek, are you all right?"

At last I came face-to-face with him. It took a moment to register what I saw.

"Ahhhhhh!" I screamed a scream so loud it almost lifted Poe's roof. I ran out of the office and down four flights of stairs, not stopping until I reached the dark woods, where Phoebe caught me in her arms.

She held me until I calmed enough to say, "He's dead. Completely dead. He's nothing but a skeleton in a custom-made suit."

"Why does that frighten you so?" Phoebe asked. "Surely one with your experience with ghosts and zombies…"

"I'm not frightened—I'm grief stricken!" I replied. "And furious. Couldn't the Tenured Ones have made Kaplan Kossek into a zombie like so many of them? Then we'd still have his genius!"

She patted my hair. "The gentleman was dead when the Tenured Ones brought him to GHU from Poland. They compensated his family for his bones. You know how they revere bones. I couldn't bring myself to tell you."

To zombies, bones were special. A zombie's flesh got eaten away, the reason many favored the bandage or mummy look. But their bones never changed. Zombie honor, however dubious, allowed them to say Kaplan Kossek resided on campus because his bones were here.

I nodded at Phoebe's words. She often haunted the faculty dining hall and eavesdropped on the Tenured Ones. She knew more about what was going on here than I did. And I should have realized that her propriety would never have permitted me to go unchaperoned for a *tête-a-tête* with Kappy if he were still alive. She was solicitous of me like that.

"But why would they want to bring him to campus dead?" Then a light went on for me. "This reminds me of Kappy's novel about an elderly villager who wins the national lottery and promptly dies of delight. The other villagers put forth an imposter to claim the winnings, which they intend on dividing among themselves. But in the end the villagers murder each other to increase their shares."

Nodding, Phoebe said, "The Tenured Ones are dividing Kaplan Kossek's substantial salary as the Edgar Allen Poe scholar." She smiled her devilish dimpled smile.

"*Avaritia est bona*," we said in unison. It was our private joke.

* * * *

But later that night I wasn't feeling so jolly. I had always been suspicious about why the English Department brought Kappy to GHU in the first place. The Tenured Ones looked down on genre fiction—mystery, romance, anything people actually read, especially horror fiction. No lyrical gory stories for them. But none for me either now that I knew Kappy was dead. I'd wanted him to inspire me to write. How would I write the great American zombie novel without Kaplan Kossek?

I couldn't stand to remain beneath his windows, so I moved my van to the Economic Department's faculty parking.

Before I went to sleep, I sneaked into Ayn Rand Hall and emailed the chair of the English Department, an androgynous person named Rutledge Browne, Rutty to his/her posse. (The English Department

Tenured Ones were so politically correct they refused to gender identify themselves or others, so everyone was a s/he.)

Normally Rutty would never read a lowly adjunct's email much less answer it. To get his/her attention, I wrote in the subject line: KAPLAN KOSSEK IS DEAD! In the body of my email I let him/her know I intended to alert the *Washington Post* about their fraud.

Along with their scheme's dishonesty, what they were doing would surely harm Kaplan Kossek's literary legacy and thus had to be unmasked. Who better to blow the whistle on them than Kappy's greatest fan?

The next morning as soon as I stepped out of my eight a.m. class, my cell phone vibrated. "Nora, dear, Rutty here. Don't be hasty. I'm sure we can come to some arrangement. How would you like a term appointment?"

At those words—term appointment—hope flooded me. This was what I always wanted. A term appointment meant I would have a full-time job for a year, which was good. It also meant I would be required to teach four comp classes a semester, not so good. But I would be paid almost a living wage, just enough to rent an efficiency apartment and get out of the cold.

"We're so impressed with your…tenacity, Nora," Rutty said. "Come to dinner this evening at the faculty dining hall, and we'll discuss your term appointment."

"Oh, thank you, Dr. Browne." I hated the eagerness in my voice. "I'll be there."

"But until then, Nora, no *Washington Post*. Is that understood?"

* * * *

That night I walked through the woods to the faculty dining hall wearing high heels and a dress I'd bought at a thrift shop especially for the occasion. I was so excited.

Although finding Kaplan Kossek dead discouraged my writing ambitions, perhaps it would turn out to be my big break in academia. I didn't fool myself, though. I knew I would have to agree to keep their secret in order to get my term appointment, which would be a bargain with the devil.

Rutty was waiting for me at the door. "Tonight just the English Department's tenured faculty members are here," s/he told me and ushered me into the large room lit only by candlelight. All the tables were pushed back against the walls, and the Tenured Ones were seated around the periphery.

For the first time in all my years at GHU, I was greeted by name by English Department luminaries, some human, some zombie, but all experts in subjects such as Shakespearean feminist deconstruction theory, the metaphysical bisexual symbolism in Joyce's *Finnegan's Wake*, and the rhetorical pedagogy of heuristics made algorithmic.

Rutty led me to the center of the room, where something crinkled under me. I looked down and noticed I was standing on a large piece of heavy plastic.

Rutty slid away from me.

Gazing around the room, I saw that the Tenured Ones had all come to their feet. I smiled back at them until I noticed that every one of them held a large stone in one hand. A killing stone.

I had always said this job would kill me. Being stoned to death wasn't quite what I expected, but it was about to happen if I didn't escape.

I started for the door, but Rutty jerked me back. When I tried slipping between the tables, the Tenured Ones closed ranks. I was trapped.

I realized they'd put the plastic sheet under me so my blood didn't stain the carpet woven in gold and green, GHU's colors. How carefully they had planned my death. For the first time ever, they set aside all their bickering and backbiting to act as one. Eliminating me had brought them unity, but I found cold comfort in this.

So I turned to face them, preparing to meet my fate when I noticed a beautiful woman in a maid's uniform going among them, filling their wine glasses. Phoebe! A trickle of hope opened inside me.

"Before we attend to the business at hand, let's toast to Adjunct Nora." Rutty looked out at his/her colleagues. "We owe a debt of gratitude to Nora and other minions who want to teach at universities so badly they're willing to do it for free. Well, almost free." This evoked a smattering of chuckles. "Because of these lesser ones, we avoid the unsavory task of teaching in order to dedicate ourselves to intellectual pursuits."

"Here, here," they said in unison. "To Nora and adjuncts everywhere!" They lifted their cups and drank.

As I looked around at their shadowy forms in the candlelight, I realized they all had similar physiques. They were stubby, big-footed, and broad-shouldered from jumping on each others' backs to get ahead. How mighty and powerful they appeared, this tribe of Tenured Ones.

But like Rome, they fell. All around me, they began to fall—even the zombies. In fact they fell faster than the living. What a glorious sight! Tossing their tumblers, slumping onto the floor, or back into their chairs, cracking their heads on the tables, they went down. Rutty sank into a puddle near me, the stone s/he had been hiding sinking with him/her.

In a flash Phoebe appeared beside me and took my hand. "We must make haste and leave this unholy place!"

I followed in her wake as we wound our way around the tables and bodies.

"My sleeping potion doesn't last long on folks who imbibe spirits the way some of these do," Phoebe said.

Behind us, we already heard moaning. Rutty was coming around.

Outside the dining hall's glass doors, Phoebe uprooted the FACULTY ONLY sign. "Help me," she said. We threaded the sign through the door's handles.

"Surely that'll hold them," I told her.

She didn't look convinced and urged me to run with her. The blanket of darkness covering campus didn't slow us down. We knew this place by heart. We were halfway up the winding path to Ayn Rand Hall when we heard them breaking open the glass doors.

From a burlap sack, Phoebe took two bottles of canola oil. "Pour," she said, handing me one. Streams of oil flowed down the path, making it as slippery as Rutty's promises.

We were almost home free when Phoebe presented me with a pouch filled with hundred-dollar bills—Ben Franklin, my favorite patriot, smiled from their centers. "This ought to sustain you until you can find suitable employment for a young lady of your talent," she said.

"But where did you get...?" I looked up into the lobby of Ayn Rand Hall, where the life-size statue of George Henry stood beside an empty wall. The Econ Department's solid gold plaque was gone.

Phoebe was smiling her dimpled smile. *"Avaritia est bona!"* we said in unison.

The Tenured Ones were getting closer. We could hear them chanting, "Nora! Nora!" They were carrying fiery torches and marching up the path toward us.

"Never fear. George will stop them." Phoebe went inside the lobby and grabbed George Henry's statue. She was a strong ghost. I held the door for her.

"Now get in your metal carriage and go."

We hugged. I wasn't sorry to leave this place or this job, but I hated to leave her. "Me too," she said without me having to say anything. She shoved me toward the parking lot.

I ran to my van, started the engine, and took off for the exit.

I was pulling out of campus when I took a last look in my rearview mirror. At the top of the hill, Phoebe had turned George Henry on his side and given him a good push. He was rolling down the path, bowling over those in the front of the mob. When their torches hit the canola oil, they burst into flames. Their screams filled the night. How ironic for a penniless adjunct to owe her life to George Henry, the patron saint of greed.

I drank in the scene and realized that perhaps now I could write my lyrical gory story after all.

Ellen Herbert's short stories have been published in *First for Women*, the *Sonora Review*, and other magazines and have won more than ten awards, including a PEN Syndicate Fiction Prize and a Virginia Fiction Fellowship. One of her stories was read on NPR's "The Sound of Writing." Her short story collection, *Falling Women and Other Stories*, will be published by Shelfstealers Publishing in 2012. Ellen's personal narratives have appeared in the *Washington Post*, the *Rambler*, and other magazines. Ellen teaches fiction at Marymount University and creative nonfiction at the Writer's Center in Bethesda, Maryland.

AN EDUCATION IN MURDER
by Smita Harish Jain

George Lewis wanted to be president of Hathaway College—feared, respected, idolized, maybe even lusted after. He would have made it, too; but only days before the Board of Trustees was to make the announcement, George Lewis turned up dead in his office, in the middle of his final act as chair of the Business Department: turning his own program from an academic success story to one that catered to the GED set.

I had been chief of the Boswell County Police Department for just over a year. Boswell was a one-horse town, and that horse was the college. The mayor had made it clear when he hired me that I was to make myself available to them 24-7. My biggest concern until today was making sure students didn't park in faculty spots. Even a student protest was just a distant possibility on this unusually quiet rural campus. I came here for the quiet lifestyle, the spectacular scenery, the calm waters, the breathtaking mountains. I came here because it was the kind of place where I could settle down with someone, someone like Annette.

When I got to Dillard Hall, George still sat in his red leather gentleman's chair, his head resting on a matching walnut flat-top desk. Blood spatters covered the first-edition hardcover books that lined the wall next to the palladian window; bits of brain clung to the wicker chair by a shelf of academic journals. Fragments of his skull lay scattered under the lowboy behind his desk; and even his antique ceiling lamp had caught clumps of blood-matted hair. Whoever did this to George really meant business.

"Steve, let us through!"

"We have a right to be here."

"Out of our way!"

I turned to find the entire faculty of the Business Department gathered outside George's office. Eggheads, the whole lot of them. I didn't know how Annette stood it. "We're PhDs; that means we're smart doctors, not rich ones," they liked to say. Then they'd laugh, as if being poor made them seem smarter to anyone. They lined up behind the yellow police tape that separated George's office from onlookers. Some had come to gawk; others just to make sure.

"Murder. It's definitely murder," Professor Calibri proclaimed as I scraped what was probably a part of George's temporal lobe off the ottoman in front of his button-tufted wing accent chair. Master of the obvious, that guy. Calibri was smart enough to have a PhD in something I couldn't spell, but too stupid to realize that he was a prime suspect. They all were. What George had planned for them was enough to drive any one of them to murder.

"The way I see it is this," Calibri continued. "George had alienated many of his colleagues in the short time he was here. One of them must have exacted their revenge for his perfidiousness."

Thanks for that insight, whatever it means.

The faculty crowded outside the door, each espousing his or her theory about what had happened in George's office. The fact that they had no training in criminal investigation seemed beside the point.

"You know, Steve," Sylvia Jones began as my team continued working the crime scene.

"*It's Chief,*" I wanted to say. I gritted my teeth. God help me if I ever called them anything but "Professor" or "Doctor."

"Yes, Dr. Jones," I said, not turning to look at her, hoping that would tell her I wasn't interested in hearing the rest.

"I think that whoever did this really hated George. I mean, look at this mess!"

More of the obvious.

"He had it coming! Everyone knows what he was doing here," Professor Mancini chimed in.

"Yes."

"That's for sure."

"Son of a bitch."

"The very idea!" came the chorus of responses from the other faculty.

They were right about one thing. What George was doing was unheard of in academia. Many considered it sacrilege, a broken promise, a giant step backward for education. On the evening of his murder, George Lewis was putting the final touches on his plan to dissolve tenure in the Business Department and convert the entire curriculum into a high-volume, certificate-granting program.

Gary Brewster couldn't keep the disdain out of his voice as he described his future at Hathaway College. "Can you believe it? Asking us, PhDs, to teach non-degree-seeking students! Who cares how much revenue it would generate? Tourism and Retail Management aren't even real majors!"

"You don't need college to do any of those jobs," Doug Mancini complained.

"That's just the point; we weren't going to be part of the *real* college anymore!" Herb Schwartz reminded him.

"I didn't go to school for nine extra years to teach future travel agents!" Marcia Paulson snorted and stormed away.

"He was even going to have us teaching online. How do you teach students if they aren't in front of you?" Thomas wondered.

It went on, but I stopped noting who said what. As far as I was concerned, they were all saying the same thing: every one of them had a reason to want George gone.

"Some of us would be going part-time! I haven't done that since I was a visiting professor! What nerve!" someone else piped up.

I shook my head and kept working.

"It's not like we're paid that much; guaranteed lifetime employment is so little to give us in exchange for all that we do," the same voice complained.

There it was. "All that we do." The Arts and Sciences faculty, long disgruntled at the significantly higher salaries that went to the Business faculty, always complained that they didn't do enough to warrant those salaries. Their research and scholarship was sketchy at best and non-existent at worst. They called the Business folks unproductive, interlopers, not of the academy.

Now they would call them murderers.

I dropped what I was doing and turned to face the crowd. I looked around for Annette but didn't see her. Surely she had heard the news by now.

"Okay, let's have everyone step into Room 410. Once we're done here, I'll be in to talk to each of you." I motioned to one of my officers to escort the Business faculty and their opinions to another room.

* * * *

An hour later, we finished processing the murder scene, and I had George Lewis's body transported to the morgue. I left one of my officers posted outside his office, in case any students showed up, and went to interview the first witness.

The cleaning woman who had found George was waiting for me in Dillard 415. One of the smaller classrooms used by the Business Department, it also doubled as the department's conference room. A collection of wooden desks pushed together into the center of the room passed for a conference table. Lecture notes from the accounting class the day before filled the blackboard: debits near the window, credits near the door. In the front of the room, an electronic whiteboard occupied the place of honor, the last vestige of a once not-so-bad program. In the two years George had served as chair of the Business Department, he took it from number five in the state to dead last. Just where he wanted it. The easiest way to dismantle a program was to show it wasn't successful.

Sitting in a metal folding chair under the only window in the room was a petite, dark-skinned woman. Her eyes were closed, her face cupped in both hands.

"Miss," I started and searched her uniform for a name tag. "Rosa. I'm Chief Summers."

She opened her eyes slowly and looked around the room, as if to remind herself where she was. She took in a long, deep breath that filled her whole chest and held it there for several seconds. When she finally exhaled, tears started down her cheeks. She sobbed quietly for a few minutes, then crossed herself and told me what had happened that morning.

She found George's body at six a.m., her usual time to clean his office on Saturdays. She unlocked his door and, after looking inside, ran screaming from the room. She never entered the office or touched anything besides the doorknob. She called the police, and we came right away. She had been waiting in Room 415 for two hours, because that's what "the boy with the uniform" told her to do. I assumed she meant one of my younger officers and didn't question her about it further. Coupled with the medical examiner's preliminary estimate that George had died about twelve hours before he was found, I could place his death at approximately six p.m. on Friday evening—a dead time in any academic building. No pun intended.

I sent her home with the assurance that she would not be asked to clean George's office, that that job belonged to trained crime-scene clean-up crews, and made my way across the hall to Room 410. The professors should have the case solved for me by now. I sighed.

"Steve! There you are. Do you have any idea how long you've left us in here?" one of them chided.

"Yes, we have other things to do," another one said.

"Is this going to take long?" the complaining continued.

Yes, George's death must be such an inconvenience for you.

I turned without responding and asked my deputy to escort the professors one by one to Room 400, where I would question each one.

Dillard 400 was a large classroom with lecture-hall seating. Many of the chairs were either broken or missing. Students had declared their love or immortalized the words to their favorite songs on the tops of the fixed tables. Some of the whiteboards could no longer be erased. Over the past two years, it, like most of the bigger classrooms in the building, had fallen into disrepair, through lack of regular use and maintenance. With the number of Business majors at an all-time low, class sizes had never been smaller.

The first faculty member in was Marcia Paulson. She took the chair at the front of the classroom, no doubt used to being the focus of the room.

"Dr. Paulson, can you tell me your whereabouts yesterday evening, around six p.m.?" I began.

Paulson huffed. She ran both hands through her gray-streaked hair and shook her head several times to make it all fall back into place. Then, with squared shoulders and a firm glare, she said, "I don't understand why you're questioning any of us. We're PhDs, not murderers."

I replied with the obvious. "Every one of you hated George Lewis's plans for the Business Department. Wouldn't some of you want to get even?"

She thought for a moment before replying. "You're right; but murder is beneath us. Besides, we were all at the meeting."

"What meeting?" I asked.

"The meeting to develop a plan to stop the destruction of the Business Department."

"Really? What's the plan?"

"We were still working on it, but murder was not on the agenda, I can assure you." She smiled. "It doesn't matter now; someone has already solved our problem."

She raised her eyebrows and waited. When I didn't take the bait, she went on anyway.

"You're not going to want to hear this, but the person you should be talking to is Annette."

"Annette?" I acted sufficiently surprised.

"She was the last one here with George last night. Just ask Doug Mancini."

It was no secret how I felt about George's secretary, Annette. What I didn't know was how much everyone else's knowing would impact my investigation. Rather than react to Paulson's insinuation, I told her she could leave and asked my deputy to bring Doug Mancini to me.

Mancini stormed in all fire and brimstone. "If you think you're going to pin this on me, you're nuts! Yes, I hated him. Who didn't? But when I left here last night, George was still alive; and I was at the SOD meeting until one a.m."

"SOD?"

"Save Our Department."

Mancini loomed over me waiting for my response.

I swallowed a smart remark about academics and their ridiculous acronyms and said, instead, "But you saw George Lewis last night, *before* the meeting?"

His bravado waned as he stammered out his response. "Yes, well, I wasn't here long, and, we just had some business to go over, and, you know—he was alive when I left!"

"Why don't you tell me exactly what happened yesterday evening, Professor Mancini."

He released a long sigh and found his way to one of the student chairs.

"Look, Annette's going to tell you that I threatened George, but she's the one with the bigger motive here. We all knew she was sleeping with him, and he was planning on leaving her behind when he moved into the president's office. She had to feel used, betrayed, furious."

I knew all this. Annette had told me so herself. I hated George for what he had been doing to Annette.

"Did you threaten George Lewis, Professor Mancini?"

"I wouldn't call it a threat, exactly."

"What would you call it?"

"It was more of an observation. I just told him changing our department from a degree program into a certificate program would be a poor choice for him to make."

Yes, I'm sure that's just how you phrased it.

"Did you see Annette here last night?"

"Yes, and actually, I was surprised to see her. All she'd been talking about all week was going to her daughter's baby shower. But the way she was dressed, I thought, maybe she'd changed her mind."

"What do you mean?"

"She was wearing the ugliest muumuu I had ever seen, not at all something someone would wear to a party." He thought another moment and said, "Of course, she didn't have much reason to come to work looking good anymore."

Was he rubbing my nose in it? Assuming that even with George out of the picture, Annette wouldn't want me?

"As I was leaving, she was coming into George's office carrying all of our personnel files," Mancini said, barely able to keep the anger out of his voice. "Her file was right on top. I felt bad for her; that bastard was making her deliver her own execution papers. She was still here when I left."

"What time was that?" I asked, hoping his answer was precise enough to narrow down the time of George's murder.

"A few minutes after six p.m.," he said.

I nodded to my deputy, who escorted Doug Mancini out and brought in the next faculty member.

Eduardo Calibri—Ed for short—started babbling before he entered the room. "What have the others told you, Steve?"

I took a deep breath. "Why don't we talk about what you have to tell me, Dr. Calibri. You must have a theory about what happened."

Calibri threw his shoulders back and sat upright, grinning from ear to ear. "I've been wondering when you'd ask! We've all been talking about it, and everyone thinks your best bet is Annette."

This is going to be easier than I thought.

"Go on," I said.

"George's office was locked when the cleaning lady came in this morning. I asked her that, specifically, before coming to see you." He nodded with satisfaction.

By all means, interfere with a police investigation.

I waited for him to continue.

"Who locked the door if George was lying in there dead to the world? Who had keys to his office? George, the cleaning lady, and Annette."

"Why couldn't the killer have used George Lewis's keys?" I asked.

"Come on, Steve. Now you're just insulting us. George's keys were on his desk. I saw them myself this morning, before you shooed us all away."

Of course you did.

I had everything I needed from Calibri and sent him out with my deputy.

After three more hours of interviews with the Business Department faculty, I learned the following: George Lewis planned to hold a department meeting in two days, in which he would "make a historic announcement." Everyone knew what it was: he was dissolving all their tenure contracts and giving them renewable one-year posts in his new certificate program. They all expected that he would spend that year finding and hiring their replacements. Some of them had talked about suing or throwing his offer back in his face; but they couldn't afford an expensive lawsuit, and their chances of leaving Boswell County to teach at another college were limited, considering they had few publications on their *vitae* and even less respect, coming from the lowest-ranked business program in the state. The youngest of them were in their mid-to-late forties, too old to start over somewhere else; and their only option in town was mussel farming in the Clinch River. They were at George's mercy. Stuck. If George had lived, the SOD committee would have been little more than a group whining session, but now it gave them all an alibi.

My next stop was President Smithson's office. He had insisted on being informed at every step of my investigation, and the mayor had given me the usual order to keep him happy.

We sat in his office, just slightly less opulent than George Lewis's, and he grilled me for a solution. "So, what are you saying, Steve? You think one of my faculty did this? Do you have any idea how that's going to look?"

"No, sir. I mean, I don't know, sir. They all have alibis."

"That settles it, then. You'll just have to look somewhere else for your murderer." He rolled his chair backward and stood to escort me out.

I remained seated. "It's just that, well, their alibis are each other. It sounds way too convenient."

"Unless you can prove that they're *all* lying, you've got no choice but to move this investigation along," the president insisted.

I knew Smithson was right. I also knew what that meant. Annette.

I had left instructions with my deputy to call me as soon as she arrived at Dillard. With no message waiting for me on my phone, I decided to catch an early lunch.

The walk to the faculty/staff dining room was brisk. The December air was crisp and unforgiving. Clutches of flame azalea bushes crouched low along the path, bare branches trying to shelter their cores from the biting wind. Every kind of maple imaginable—silver, red, striped, sugar, black, and ashleaf—shivered along Campus Walk. Bigleaf magnolias yearning for spring lined the pathways between the academic quad and the rest of the buildings.

The dining room was buzzing with the news of George's murder. All of the Business faculty were there, each holding court at his or her own table, entertaining rapt listeners with what it was like to be interrogated, how George's office looked decorated with his own cranial matter, and why it was only a matter of time before Annette would be arrested.

I rose to get my third cup of coffee, when I heard the familiar ring tone I'd assigned to all my work numbers. It was my deputy. Annette Walker was in Dillard Hall.

* * * *

I waited in Dillard 400 for my deputy to bring Annette in. I couldn't sit still and paced the large room. I hadn't seen her in a week, not since I ran into her outside Washington Hall.

Annette had been coming out of her regular Friday afternoon committee meeting, and I was on my way to lunch. We walked together to the dining hall. She'd been bubbling over with the news of her daughter's baby shower—the theme, what she would wear, her gift for her first grandchild. I'd hugged her with my congratulations; she'd hugged me back.

I was thinking about the possibilities when Annette stepped into the room. I started toward her, arms outstretched, but dropped them when I saw my deputy walking in behind her.

After a quick exchange with my deputy about the results of the faculty interviews, I motioned for him to leave. He closed the door behind him. Annette remained standing, her hands clasped in front of her.

"Annie." I placed a hand on her shoulder.

She smiled weakly and sat down in one of the student desk chairs near the door.

I took a chair near her. "Annie, tell me what happened last night."

She crossed her arms over her chest and didn't look up when she spoke.

"I left here the same time I do every night, a few minutes after six p.m.," she began.

"George asked me to stay late and help him write up new contract letters, but I had Stacy and Mark's shower to go to, and the bus was leaving in less than twenty minutes. If I missed it, I would miss my connection. The party started at eight, and I wanted to leave myself plenty of time."

Annette had grown up in Manhattan, I knew, where it was too expensive and too crowded to own a car. She got used to public transportation early in her life and stuck with it. She had moved to Boswell County three years ago but still hadn't learned how to drive. Lately, George did much of her driving for her—to and from his house. I pushed that thought aside and continued with my interview.

"There were plenty of buses that would have gotten you to Stacy's by eight p.m.; what was your rush?" I asked.

"The shower got moved at the last minute from Stacy's house to one of her friend's in England Run," she explained. "Jennifer, my student aide, gave me the message. I'd never heard of the neighborhood, so I wanted to leave myself extra time to get there."

"So, plenty of people must have seen you at the party," I said, feeling this, coupled with the complicated bus routes I knew she had to take to get there, could serve as an alibi.

Her lips clamped down in a thin line.

"I never made it to the party," she said. She rubbed her temples with her fingers. "I tried asking people for directions; but no one had heard of the street. The bus dropped me off in the England Run area, and from there I had planned on walking the last few blocks. I finally stopped at someone's house to use their phone, but my daughter didn't pick up. I ended up coming home." She dabbed her eyes with a handkerchief.

"Why didn't you just use your cell phone?"

"I lost it last week, right after I saw you. I just don't know where it went. You know, this is all so strange. When I spoke to my daughter late last night, she said the shower location had never changed. Why would someone leave me a fake message like that?"

Good question.

"Annie, I'll need to know exactly which buses you took and everyone you talked to. Do you remember where the house was where you stopped?"

Annette gave me her bus route and the general location and description of the house where she had stopped to call her daughter. The other people she had talked to were simply passersby; there would be little chance of tracking them down. Still, I had something.

"What happened in George's office, Annette?"

"I didn't kill him, Steve. You know me better than that." She looked confused, as if trying to figure out if all of this was real. "I can't believe he's dead."

I tried asking her a few more questions, but she was barely holding it together.

"It'll be okay, Annie," I said, and put my arms around her. She sniffed noisily but didn't say anything. Instead, she searched my face, as if looking for a clue about what I was thinking. I wanted to tell her, but it wasn't time.

Just then, my phone rang. It was Smithson. I told Annette that I'd see her again soon and asked my deputy to drive her home. President Smithson wanted to know if I had learned anything new. I spent the next half-hour in his office filling him in.

"So, Annette killed George in a fit of rage over being rejected? Wrath of a woman scorned, huh?" Smithson said.

"Just a minute, sir. I still have leads to follow up. I'm not ready to make an arrest, yet," I said, picturing squad cars racing to Annette's house and officers dragging her away in shackles.

"Well, see that an arrest gets made soon. We've got students running around scared, parents threatening to pull their kids out, and townspeople spreading more and more rumors about what's happening at Hathaway. This is *not* how I want to end my presidency."

He dismissed me with the understanding that I would report every new detail to him as soon as I uncovered it. Of course, the news would go live the minute I left his office. He would make certain everyone knew that someone would pay for the murder. Right now, it looked as if that someone would be Annette.

* * * *

I spent the next day recreating how George Lewis's murder would have happened if Annette were the killer. I started with a visit to the student aide, a local girl, who was waiting out the investigation at home with her parents.

The four of us sat in their living room, Jennifer McNally and her parents on the sofa, me settled on a recliner in front of them.

"Jennifer, can you tell me what you remember about that phone call?"

She licked her lips before she spoke, the silver stud in her tongue visible for just a second.

"Yes, sir. I, like, remember writing down the message for Annette; she was at lunch. I mean, someone called to say that, like, her daughter's shower had changed. Then they gave me directions to, like, give to Annette."

This is, like, going to take, like, a really long time.

"Did you recognize the caller's voice?"

"No, sir. I mean, the lines are, like, really busy during lunch, and, you know, I'm the only one there. I just, like, try to get the phone calls over with as quickly as possible, you know?"

"Of course, that's understandable," I said. "Do you remember if it was a man or a woman who called?"

"No, I mean, I can't remember; there were a lot of calls yesterday."

"So, someone called, gave you directions to Stacy's baby shower, and hung up. That's it?"

She nodded.

"Jennifer, is there anything else you can think of?" I asked.

"There is, like, one thing," she said. "I, like, always look at the caller ID when a phone call comes in, you know, so I don't have to ask for the phone number. I mean, it just, like, saves me some time or whatever, you know?"

I nodded. *Like, go on.*

"Well, anyway, this call came from somewhere, like, on campus. The number was only four digits long, you know."

Yes, I know.

My interview with the student aide ended just before six p.m., leaving me enough time to make the 6:20 bus—the same bus Annette said she took the night before.

I re-traced Annette's bus route. The weekend bus schedule was the same on Friday and Saturday evenings, as were the drivers. All three remembered Annette because she had asked them several times if she was going the right way, how far away her stop was, exactly which bus she should take to make her transfer. I also stopped at the house from which she had called her daughter. The people who lived there remembered her.

"She was a pretty woman, but that dress she was wearing wasn't the least bit becoming," the wife noted.

"Pretty or not, she didn't have to behave so poorly," the husband added. "Rude, really."

Not at all Annie's personality, but, under the circumstances, understandable. She was so easily flustered.

* * * *

"That's it, then. Annette made the phone call herself, to give her a way to get out of going to the party," President Smithson decided when I briefed him in his office the next morning.

"Why would she do that, sir?" I asked. *When I could have done it just as easily. I knew she wouldn't be there, and the student aide wouldn't recognize my voice.*

"Come on, Steve. Do I have to do your job for you? She was never planning on going to the baby shower. She just told everyone she was. She made sure a couple of bus drivers and some random family remembered seeing her far away from the murder site, so she'd have an alibi. Why else would she have acted so agitated, if not to be memorable?"

Her only daughter? Her first grandchild? I can see it.

"Maybe she was just frustrated because she was lost?" I said.

"Yes, or maybe the blood residue your people found in the ladies room sink in Dillard came off of Annette's hands. How long before we know if the blood is George's?"

I can tell you now; it's George's.

"Not long, sir. But chances are pretty good it's his, since the doors to Dillard were locked at 6:15 last night. Officer Reynolds was on duty, and he recorded the time in the police log." *I had to re-lock them when I left.*

"And Annette was the last person to see George alive," he said, putting his own pieces together.

Second to last.

"But, sir, the lab results showed no blood residue on Annette's muumuu. If she had mutilated George Lewis, the medical examiner said she definitely would have been covered with his blood."

"Really, Steve, you disappoint me. A muumuu? When have you ever known Annette to wear a muumuu? I don't mind telling you, I've watched her from time to time. That woman knows how to wear clothes right." He waggled his eyebrows.

Didn't I mention the baby shower had a Hawaiian theme?

"Don't you see it, yet, Steve? All right, I'll spell it out for you. Annette was wearing a muumuu because it was easy for her to take off. The reason you didn't find any blood on her clothes was because she wasn't wearing any when she killed George. She distracted him, beat his brains out, washed up, then put her muumuu back on. My wife sleeps in one, and they're the easiest things to get in and out of, if you know what I mean."

Yes, I know what you mean.

I dropped my head into my hands and said through my fingers, "And the murder weapon, sir? What did she do with that?"

"She must have gotten rid of it that night. It's dark by five-thirty nowadays; it's not like she'd have to worry about being seen," he said, wiping his palms together to suggest a clean disposition of the matter.

You're right; a dark blue police uniform, even a blood-soaked one, would hardly be noticed in the dark. And now, all that was left of it was ashes, which, along with a steel baseball bat, were somewhere at the bottom of the Clinch River. There was no evidence left to trace anyone to George Lewis's murder.

"Not bad, not bad," Smithson said to himself and nodded. "Clever, really. I guess our little Annette is more than just a pretty face." Sherlock Holmes sat back, pleased with his own adroitness.

"It's not looking good for Annette," I said and shook my head with as much disquiet as I could feign.

* * * *

Annette's trial lasted only three days. The prosecution hammered on her motive, her access to George's office, and the fact that she was the last known person to see George alive. By the time the prosecution rested, Annette looked defeated, drained of any hope, ready to give up. She didn't know what I knew, that in my pre-trial interview with her lawyer, I had given him everything he would need to find all the holes in the case against her. When I told her, she would be so grateful.

I sat back and watched her lawyer go to work. He pointed out to the jury that all the evidence against Annette was circumstantial and that there were no eyewitnesses. He saved his trump card for last.

"Dr. Shepherd," Annette's lawyer addressed the chief medical examiner for Boswell County. "A crime of this much violence, this much anger, would you call it a crime of passion?"

"It certainly looked that way. In fact, of the eight blows inflicted, only the first was necessary to kill George Lewis. The remaining seven did nothing more than satisfy some animalistic urge in the killer."

It was certainly made to look that way.

"Let's take a look at the timeline, shall we, Dr. Shepherd?"

The lawyer didn't wait for a response. "You said earlier that such a massacre would take at least three minutes to complete and several more minutes to clean oneself up after. Professor Mancini testified that George Lewis was alive a few minutes after six o'clock, and Officer Reynolds testified that the building was locked at 6:15 p.m., so only someone with a key could have gotten in or out. Wouldn't that suggest that if Annette Walker had killed George Lewis, she had to butcher him, clean herself up so thoroughly that no blood remained on her body or clothing, lock the building, and catch the 6:20 p.m. bus at a stop that was a good twelve-minute walk from Dillard Hall, all in seventeen minutes?"

Dr. Shepherd twisted his face toward the ceiling and counted off on his fingers. The jury did the same. "Yes, that's right."

* * * *

The jury came back in just thirty minutes. Not guilty.

I smiled to myself and thought about what I would say to Annie—how happy I was for her, for us. I drove to her house and waited.

At midnight, her lawyer's car pulled up, and the two of them got out. He had one arm wrapped around a half-empty magnum of champagne and the other around Annette. The two of them, laughing, staggered into her house.

I stared at her bedroom window long after the light had gone out.

Smita Harish Jain has been working in academia for almost twenty years, which has given her lots of fodder for her writing. This isn't the first time she's killed someone...on paper.

A GRAIN OF TRUTH
by Leone Ciporin

The truth is, I don't care enough about anyone to think about killing them. I generally keep to myself. So I certainly never planned on writing a story about murder. But the idea popped into my head, and it wouldn't leave me alone.

I don't write fiction and, more importantly, I don't know where to sell it, so I pushed the thought away. I had a living to make. Planted in a sandy railroad town on the outskirts of the square states, far from the center of the literary world, I make the most of my remoteness by writing magazine articles about a neglected region.

My last assignment had not been my favorite, mainly because of an unpleasant interview with an antiques appraiser. Though the receptionist worked with all the offices on his floor, she didn't seem overworked. She peered at me above a tabloid. "Yeah?" Very professional.

"I'm here to see Will Renswick. I have an appointment." I stared pointedly at her empty desk calendar.

She waved a hand behind her. "Last one on the right."

Last one on the right was a miniscule room still reminiscing on its likely origin as a closet, with stacks of boxes covering two walls and a battered desk along a third. A small, dust-covered window offered hope of escape. The man inside looked as if he'd just crawled in through that window. Mud-splattered boots, worn jeans, and sunburned cheeks all testified to his preference for the outdoors.

"Mr. Renswick?" The room couldn't hold us both, so I stood in the hall and held out my business card. "I'm Annabelle Gilbert. I called you last week?"

He took the card. "I remember."

I pulled out my notebook. "I'm writing about Western antiques—spurs, buckles, boots. For example, the Spanish spurs, *espuela grande*—how have they been adapted?"

The man talked. And talked. Leaning against his desk, he launched into a lecture that gave me way more information than I needed. He extolled the craftsmanship of spurs and the skill of those who made them, including Oscar Crockett.

"Any relation to Davy?" I asked, mainly to stop the flow.

"Not that I know." He looked down at me through half-closed eyes. "Why aren't you home making dinner for your husband?"

I showed him my teeth. "Because I have to earn the dinner before I can cook it." I tapped my notebook. "What about today? What kind of spurs do cowboys wear?"

"Little lady, pickup trucks don't need spurs. There aren't many real cowboys today."

"There are still cows, right?" I spoke just loud enough for him to hear.

The bellow that emerged made me jump. "How dare you tell me about cowboys! Get home where you belong!" He punctuated his instruction with a door slam in my face. I avoided the receptionist's stare as I left.

I'd been glad to finish that article and move on to one on railroads, even though I was stuck on how to approach it. I pushed myself away from the computer, dumped Cat off my lap, and brushed orange fur from my knees. After Cat followed me home last year and stayed, I refused to name him Marmalade or Fluffy or Pumpkin. I named him Cat because that's what he is. I'm a nonfiction type of person.

Cat settled himself in his usual corner of the sofa as if the move had been his idea. Though my apartment is minimalist—bare floors, no pictures on the wall—after Cat arrived, I bought a lumpy, over-stuffed sofa at a garage sale. He accepted the gift without a trace of gratitude. I liked that about him.

I captured my hair into a ponytail and shrugged on a thin sweater against the morning breeze before heading down to the coffee shop. After standing in line behind two women chatting about a reality show, I eventually got my latte. Gripping my cup's cardboard sleeve, I skirted the edge of the café to sit at a table for two in the back corner. In my case, a table for one. Other customers crowded by the window, but I prefer walls. The boundaries are clearer.

I sipped my coffee and pushed my mind toward conductors and stationmasters. Then, like train cars coupling, the story idea, the Renswick interview, and the railroads connected. *Murder on the Orient Express.* Cowboy collides with caboose. Something like that.

Steamed milk dripped onto my knuckles as I trotted back to my apartment. My fingers couldn't hit the keyboard fast enough. I churned through search engines to see how killing someone and tossing them off a train could look like an accident. I came across references to bodies found near train tracks over the past several years, along with cargo thefts where police suspected a group of transients. I put the two together and patterned my crime like a gang killing, so the murderer could blame it on the gang. The cargo thieves had never been caught, so I looked up local gangs and learned all about them: the Hobo Gang with their black bandannas, the Losers with their snake tattoos, and even a gang that only took in guys who had already been in prison. Ideas snapped into place, and I alternated between the Internet and the story, folding in the search results as my plot hit critical points.

By midnight, the tips of my fingers were sore, my brain felt pleasantly emptied, and a passable draft stared back at me. I saved it to my hard drive and launched myself onto my bed, so tired I fell asleep in midair.

After I finished my railroad article, I re-read my murder story. Half-decent. Fully decent for my first try at fiction. By the end of the week, I'd begun exploring fiction markets to find out who'd pay me for it.

Saturday afternoon, two plainclothes cops showed up at my door. One was tall and very nice looking; the other was short and somewhat wide. The tall one spoke. "Ms. Gilbert? Annabelle Gilbert?"

At my nod, they flashed badges and the tall one said, "I'm Detective Brogan and this is Detective Short." I didn't smother my laugh fast enough, and Short glared at me. Brogan asked, "Do you know a Willard Renswick?"

Oh, no. Whatever he'd done, I did not want to be involved.

"I don't think so. Why?"

Brogan looked at me through tangled blond lashes, then at my apartment. I took the hint. "Would you like to come in?" I asked. They walked in before I finished the sentence. As they scanned the apartment, I was grateful for its neatness, but, watching Brogan stride across the room, I regretted not losing those ten extra pounds.

Brogan perched on the edge of the sofa while Short stood next to it, his head now slightly above Brogan's. Cat, displaced from his spot, watched from the kitchen, tail twitching.

I sat in my desk chair and swiveled to face them, wishing I'd worn a skirt. "What can I do for you?" I asked. What had Renswick done?

"Are you sure you don't know him?" Short said.

"No, I'm not sure. I meet a lot of people."

Brogan raked a hand through short hair. "How so?" He softened the question with a smile from bright blue eyes.

My anxiety began to blend with a different kind of excitement. I don't meet many men with eyes like his. "I'm a freelance writer, mostly articles on the Old West, that kind of thing." A strand of hair wandered into my mouth, and I pushed it aside. "So I interview people." I stabbed a glance at Short. "I'm careful to get my facts straight."

"Mr. Renswick was found dead earlier today," Short said. "His wallet was gone, but your business card was in his pocket."

No way I could stay uninvolved now. "Dead? And he had *my* business card? What does—did—he do for a living?"

Brogan flipped open a notebook. "Antiques appraiser." He ran a finger down his notes. "Also worked on a ranch." A real cowboy, after all.

I nodded. "Oh. The antiques guy. I interviewed him about an article on Old West artifacts."

Short had moved next to me. He pointed to my desk. "You've got a lot of material here on trains."

As I tilted my head to face Short, I saw Brogan's mouth twitch. Not a flirtatious twitch. Uh oh. "I just finished an article on railroads for a travel magazine," I said.

Short's black eyes glimmered. "Mind if we take a look?"

Shark-movie music played in my head as I pulled up the article and wheeled back to let Short shuffle closer. His bulbous nose nearly touched the screen. Brogan crossed the room to lean in behind him, his taller frame forming a second quote mark around Short's body. Brogan's eyes formed slits and his square jaw moved back and forth. I wasn't sure he was cute anymore.

The two men straightened in unison. Brogan flicked a glance at Short, who mumbled goodbye and left. Returning to the sofa, Brogan sat on its corner and asked, "When did you meet with Renswick?"

I spread my palms. "A few weeks ago, I guess."

"But you didn't remember him."

I abandoned being agreeable. "I didn't remember his *name*. Look, what's going on here? You said this guy Renswick was found dead? How did he die?" I was betting his wife had done it. "What does any of this have to do with me?"

Brogan aimed his beautiful eyes at me. "He was murdered. His head cracked open and his body thrown by the train tracks just east of here."

Goose bumps crawled up my arms. "Train tracks?" Nausea now joined the goose bumps for a plague-like effect.

He lowered his head to stare at me from the roof of his eyes. "I have a few more questions." Brogan peppered me with queries on my background before getting up to leave. Despite the eyes, I was glad to see him go.

When Short returned with a warrant for my computer, I nearly cried watching my livelihood disappear down the stairs. As soon as he left, I looked up lawyers, called the one with the biggest ad, and made an appointment.

* * * *

Frank Gaston's office resembled an anthill, with phones ringing, keyboards clicking, people trotting the hallway. Though I saw only four people, they seemed like a hundred. After the din outside, his private office seemed like a retreat, with white walls, an occasional photograph, neat bookshelves, and a spotless desk.

He motioned me to sit. "You're taller than I expected." His voice carried a reassuring rumble.

"What did you expect?" I slid my purse down by my chair.

"I heard that Brogan called you 'petite.'"

My cheeks burned. "You've been talking to the cops?"

"I have a contact there. I like to know what I'm getting into." He leaned back. "They think you did it. There's some incriminating stuff on your computer, and Renswick's receptionist said you and he weren't exactly buddies."

A concrete block landed in my stomach. I didn't see the leap of logic from my arguing with Renswick to my murdering him, but a jury might.

"I didn't do it." I explained about the interview, my railroads article, and my mystery story. He told me not to say anything when they arrested me, except to ask for a phone to call him.

A few days later, as Gaston predicted, Short arrested me. The clincher was my computer, my research on train murders, traced through cookies, the footprints computers leave behind. The cops pulled up my searches on past train murders, forensics sites on how to kill someone, law enforcement sites outlining homicide investigation techniques. Gaston told them about my mystery story, which, of course, the cops found on my computer, but they must have thought I'd killed Renswick and then written about it—committing murder and then trying to make money off it. I was annoyed that they thought I'd be that stupid.

So I ended up in the county jail in an orange jumpsuit. All the other inmates wore one, too, so no one-upping each other in fashion. I shared a room of bunk beds with ten other women, each with her own rehearsed defense. A roomful of story leads. If I ever got out.

Gaston had told me the police found black fibers under Renswick's fingernails. Renswick had probably clawed at his attacker, so the fibers could be from the killer's shirt or...I remembered the Hobo Gang wore black bandannas. Could that be it?

Thanks to a pending civil liberties lawsuit, the county was experimenting with limited Internet access for legal research. They'd blocked the best sites, allowed only an hour a day, and had a guard pacing the room, but I took full advantage of it. Research is my business, and I'm good at it.

I searched the web for arrests and incidents close to the train tracks and found an article on the recent arrest of a drifter named Randy Bonner on assault charges. His mug shot showed a torn black bandanna around his neck. Yes!

I alerted Gaston. He seemed less than impressed, telling me, "Plenty of bandannas around." But I pressed him to let me talk to Brogan, enduring a flood of caveats, cautions, and objections before he finally agreed.

Brogan would have been a fine sight in any event, but he was especially dazzling after staring at gray jailhouse walls. I wanted to swim laps in those eyes.

"You wanted to see me?" Brogan leaned back in his chair in the stark interview room like he was in someone's comfortable living room. His eyes drifted from me to Gaston and back. "Ready to confess?"

"If I ever do anything worth confessing, I'll let you know." Then I laid out the documents I'd printed and ran through how I'd found Bonner. He picked up each one as I spoke, eventually shepherding them into one neat pile. "I'll look into it."

After several more days with my life hovered on pause, he matched Bonner's bandanna with the fibers caught in Renswick's fingernails, and I became a free woman. Brogan met me at the jail entrance with my computer, offered me a ride, and said to call if I needed anything.

I grinned into his blue eyes. "I love Italian food." If I started writing mysteries, I'd need a cop for a friend. Especially a cute cop.

When he dropped me off, I handed him my card, and he gave me a sideways smile, holding up my card with two fingers as I shut the door.

The next morning, I celebrated my freedom with a visit to the coffee shop. Brushing pastry crumbs off the newspaper story on Bonner's upcoming arraignment, I tried to feel sorry for the dead Renswick, but not a finger of pity crossed my heart. Instead, I leaned against the wall, hooked my jeans around the chair legs and, holding my cup in a salute, I toasted myself with a victory latte.

The way things had turned out, I'd have no problem selling my story.

When she's not writing mysteries, Leone Ciporin works in public affairs for an insurance company. Her short story "A Rose by Any Other Name" was published in *Chesapeake Crimes II,* and several of her mini-mysteries have been published in *Woman's World* magazine. A member of Sisters in Crime and Mystery Writers of America, Leone lives in Virginia.

MIKED FOR MURDER
by Cathy Wiley

Katie Hawkins stared in horror at the dead body on the meeting room floor. "This is definitely *not* on the agenda."

She had come in mega early to check the room setup before The Client From Hell arrived. Everything had to be perfect, or Katie would never hear the end of it.

A dead body *wasn't* perfect. And she knew the client would blame her for this. She shook her head in shame at that thought; she should be more concerned about this poor man.

Katie headed for the phone on the wall, then paused. The room was a potential crime scene, and she might contaminate it. She was a devotee of crime shows on television, so she knew the cops always complained when a civilian tromped all over their evidence.

Backing out quickly, she screamed as she bumped into something solid. She pivoted, risking breaking the heels on her fashionable but uncomfortable shoes. Relief flowed through her. The obstacle was Chad Bentley, her boss and general manager of the Two Palms Hotel.

She dropped her clipboard and gripped both of his shoulders. "Chad! There's a body in there! I think he's dead."

Chad never panicked. Katie prided herself in her ability to remain calm when things were falling apart around her, but she could never reach the same level of unflappability as her boss.

Chad flicked placid hazel eyes toward the door of the Grand Ballroom. "A dead body? I know Baltimore has a high murder rate, but we've managed to avoid it here."

"Why do you assume it's murder?"

He glanced at his wristwatch. "It's not even six o'clock, Katie. No one should be in that room this early other than Bobby. And you would have said if the body was Bobby's."

"No, it's not Bobby." Even with just a quick view, Katie knew the body wasn't her banquet captain.

"Therefore anyone inside must be there for nefarious purposes. So if he or she is dead, I doubt it's from natural causes."

"He, I think. And yeah, he's dead." She shuddered remembering the sight...and smell.

Chad went to open the door, but Katie grabbed his arm. He stopped and glanced back, one dark eyebrow raised.

"Don't you watch *CSI*? You shouldn't touch the door. You could get fingerprints on it, or mess up the ones that are already there."

Chad removed a turquoise handkerchief from his suit pocket and used it to push open the door. Perhaps the slightest bit of emotion passed over his face as he stared at the body. "Yes, Katie, I think you're right. Definitely dead." He wrinkled his nose. "Died badly too, by the smell of it. Got your cell phone on you?"

Katie smacked herself in the forehead. Why hadn't she thought about using her cell phone? She pulled it out of her pocket and dialed 911.

She had just finished giving the details to the operator when the Client From Hell strode off the elevator and headed toward the registration table located just outside the ballroom door.

Katie ran over to intercept Mrs. Rudy halfway. "Mrs. Rudy, how good to see you! We still need to finalize the menu for tonight's reception, I believe. Why don't we go into my office and do that?" Katie gently gripped Mrs. Rudy's arm and tried to steer her away.

"My word, Ms. Hawkins." The bird-thin woman complained as she easily shrugged off Katie's hand and headed for the table. "Let me put down my registration packets, at least. And what do you mean 'finalize the menu'? We took care of that *months* ago."

Katie looked desperately at Chad, but he just shrugged and left it up to her. She took a deep breath. "Well, that's true. But the... the shrimp didn't come in on time, so we need to substitute another appetizer."

That got Mrs. Rudy's attention. "What? You promised me that we'd have plenty of shrimp cocktail. We definitely need to discuss this. But first, there are handouts that need to be distributed to each seat. Plus I need to straighten out these name tags. Who moved them?"

"Let me take care of those for you, Mrs. Rudy," Chad said smoothly, taking the box from the woman. "I assume the handouts are inside. I'll get our banquet staff to see to that right away." He quirked a brow at Katie.

It took Katie a moment to interpret his expression. Where *was* the banquet staff? Although the servers wouldn't show up until seven, Bobby should already be there making certain all the audio-visual equipment was up and running. She knew he had worked the night before, flipping the room set-up from the previous meeting, but Bobby could be relied upon to be there bright and early. Hopefully Chad would find him.

Chad set the handouts down outside the door before walking to the main hallway. Katie could hear him paging Bobby on the radio.

Katie kept one ear open to hear if Bobby answered as she listened to Mrs. Rudy drone on about the day's agenda. The same agenda they had gone over on the phone, on email, during the pre-con meeting, and again the night before when Mrs. Rudy came over to make certain the room was set up correctly.

She made understanding noises at Mrs. Rudy while noting that Bobby had not answered the radio call. Chad walked by her, heading toward the AV closet where Bobby had his office.

Katie was stuck. She wanted to get Mrs. Rudy out of the foyer, but she had to wait for the police. She crossed her fingers and hoped that Chad would come back to relieve her before the police arrived.

First, she needed to convince Mrs. Rudy to stop re-aligning the nametags. The woman shouldn't be touching anything, Katie thought. Without getting closer—a thought Katie didn't want to contemplate—there was no way to tell how the man on the ballroom floor had died, so anything could be evidence.

Katie considered the plastic name tags on the table. The plastic badge holder was made of flimsy plastic, definitely not strong or sharp enough to stab through skin, much less flesh, plus she hadn't seen any blood around the body, just...bodily fluids. She supposed the lanyard could be used to strangle someone.

Glancing back toward the ballroom, she wondered who the victim was. She knew it wasn't Bobby from the body's light skin tone.

Chad came hurrying back. Katie felt relief that she'd be able to leave the ballroom and the police in his hands while she got Mrs. Rudy out of the way. When Chad crooked a finger at her, it was her turn to raise an eyebrow at him as she stepped away from the registration table.

"I found Bobby," he whispered.

"And?"

"He was in the AV room. Tied up and gagged. After I untied him, I told him to stay put."

"Oh, my God."

"He said someone knocked him out last night," Chad continued. "I assume it has something to do with our friend in the ballroom."

Katie barely had time to digest that before Mrs. Rudy spoke up.

"There's someone in the ballroom?" The woman straightened, smoothing the crease out of her stark black suit. "Your hotel promised that the ballroom would be locked up at all times. We have proprietary information in there that shouldn't be seen by anyone not approved."

"That's not going to be a problem, Mrs. Rudy," Katie said and breathed a sigh of both relief and resignation when two uniformed police officers stepped off the elevator. "The gentleman in the ballroom is in no position to divulge any classified material. Right this way, officers."

She opened the door, attempting to let the police officers in without giving Mrs. Rudy a chance to see inside. No such luck.

"Who's that? My God, is someone dead? How? What's that smell?"

"We haven't determined who the victim is yet, but yes, it appears that there has been a death in that room. We don't know how the person got in or how he died," Katie said in one breath. She didn't bother answering the question about the smell.

"Mr. Cervantes promised he'd lock up yesterday after I left," Mrs. Rudy protested, peeking around Katie, trying to get a closer view.

It took Katie a moment to remember that Mr. Cervantes was Bobby.

"Yes, well, I'm sure he meant to," Chad said. "However, someone knocked him out before he had the chance."

Before he could continue, Mrs. Rudy shoved past Chad, took several steps into the room, stopped short, and, much to Katie's surprise, burst into tears. She hadn't thought the woman was all that fond of Bobby, or anyone on their staff, for that matter. She'd never known Mrs. Rudy to show any emotion other than anger or condescension. But there she was, crying over one of the hotel's employees. Katie put a comforting arm around the weeping woman and escorted her out of the room. For the first time, Katie felt a sense of connection with her client. Perhaps she had judged her too harshly before. Mrs. Rudy might even be—

"That's my husband," Mrs. Rudy sobbed as she accepted Chad's handkerchief.

Katie gasped, comprehension dawning. "Your husband?" As she stared through the open door, she could see the police officers around the body. One of them was on his radio, the other crouched near the victim. "How can you tell?"

"That's Lou's toupee. I'd recognize it anywhere." Mrs. Rudy collapsed into one of the chairs and laid her head on the table.

Katie stared at the body. Now that she focused on the hair, she could tell it was a toupee. Could you identify a body through its hairpiece, she wondered? "Excuse me, officers," she called out.

One of them stepped out of the room to speak with her. "Yes, ma'am?"

"Two things. First of all, Mrs. Rudy believes she can identify your victim. And we have a potential witness waiting in the AV room."

"Thank you, ma'am." He gestured to the other officer to come join them. "We've contacted Homicide and the detectives should be here soon. I'll go secure the potential witness. My partner can escort Mrs. Rudy to ID the victim."

Before Katie could direct him to the AV room, a scream rent the air. Katie winced as Isadora Amaya, one of her banquet servers, ran out the door toward her, screeching. Katie gathered the hysterical young woman in her arms.

"How the hell did *she* get in there? I thought we secured these doors," the first officer complained.

"Back door to the server's hallway," Katie explained. "So they can get in and out to serve during functions." She turned her focus to the woman. "I'm so sorry, Isa. Easy, just breathe deeply. Come with me, and let's get some tea."

She escorted Isa to the break area, fetched her a cup of hot, generously sugared tea, then flagged down another server to escort Isa to the meeting office. Then Katie headed back to the ballroom to find out if the victim was, in fact, Mrs. Rudy's husband. If it was, she felt sorry for him. She felt sorry for any man married to that—

Katie bit her lip and chastised herself for being so harsh. Mrs. Rudy was a widow now, after all. Additional wails coming from inside the ballroom seemed to confirm that fact.

Mrs. Rudy staggered back out, being supported by a police officer. She plopped into a chair by the sign-in table and wiped away her tears with Chad's handkerchief. "Yes, that's Lou," she said. "I'm sorry. I usually don't lose control like this. It's just, it's been a bad time for Lou and me. In fact, we're in the process of getting a divorce." She sniffled. "Well, we *were* in the process."

Katie felt a surge of sympathy for the woman. Perhaps this was the reason she had been so hard to work with.

Mrs. Rudy turned to Katie. "I hope you're not charging *me* for the tea you gave that waitress, Ms. Hawkins."

The sympathy dried up. "You won't be charged." *And it's a banquet server, not a waitress.*

"I can't imagine why Lou was here," Mrs. Rudy continued. "He doesn't normally attend my meetings. That's one reason we're getting divorced. He refuses to support me in the projects that are so important to me."

Katie waited to see if the police officer was going to ask more questions, but he seemed to be just guarding the door, waiting for Homicide. That didn't mean *she* couldn't ask questions.

"So." Katie tried to sound more sympathetic than interrogative. "What did Lou...Mr. Rudy...your husband do?"

"He was an artist," she sniffled. "A talented leather worker. Made purses, belts, vests."

Katie nodded, wondering how an artist ended up married to such a demanding, anal person. She heard the elevator *ding* and looked over to see two men walking down the hallway toward them. Both men were striking. The shorter man was burly and deeply tanned and the other…well, Greek god came to Katie's mind. Blond hair, blue eyes, broad shoulders. She noticed Chad checking out the hottie as well. She sighed. She and her boss had such similar taste in men. Even worse, from Katie's point of view, Chad was four for five out of the men they'd both been attracted to. But what could she expect when she took a job in Mount Vernon, the Greenwich Village of Baltimore?

The blond held up his badge. "Detective Wertz." Nodding to the man next to him, he continued. "And this is Detective Garcia."

Katie caught Detective Garcia leering at her. Well, she reasoned, at least he'd be available, since he was ogling her and not Chad. Not that Katie was interested. Garcia's leer repulsed her.

Katie offered a hand to Detective Wertz. "I'm Katie Hawkins, director of the hotel's executive meeting center. This is Chad Bentley, the hotel's general manager, and Mrs. Glenda Rudy, my client." She panicked when she wondered if she should have introduced her client first. "Mrs. Rudy is also the wife of the victim."

Neither detective seemed to react to that, so she decided to press on. "I'm the one who found the body this morning, at about 5:45. Chad came in about two minutes later. Mrs. Rudy showed up about ten minutes after that. We also discovered that someone attacked our banquet captain, Bobby, sorry, Roberto Cervantes, last night. Chad found him bound and gagged in the AV room."

"Have either of you touched the body or altered anything?" Detective Wertz asked.

"Well, we tried to keep everyone out. I only had taken two or three steps inside when I first spotted the body, and I quickly backed out of the room. But then Mrs. Rudy thought she recognized her husband and walked in a few feet. And one of our banquet servers came in the back door and ran screaming through the room. I'm not sure if she, um, we…contaminated the scene."

"Do you have surveillance cameras for this area?" the detective asked, scanning the room.

"Only at the elevators," Chad answered. "Downstairs in our lobby and restaurant we have more cameras, but not on the other floors. Our customers prefer more privacy."

Katie admired Chad's clever explanation. He made the lack of cameras sound like a benefit, rather than the hotel's reluctance to shell out money for additional security cameras.

"Mr. Bentley, we'll need copies of the visuals from all the cameras in the vicinity," Wertz said. "Now, we'd appreciate it if you could take Detective Garcia to speak with the banquet captain."

After the two men left, Wertz turned to Mrs. Rudy. "Ma'am, if you could wait here for a moment, I'll need to talk to you."

After her nod, he walked over to the police officer on guard. "What do we have?"

Katie strained to hear and caught the words "vomiting, poison, nasty." She had to agree with the latter. The body appeared to have voided itself completely, which had accounted for the smell.

The detective started to close the ballroom door. She hurried forward. "Excuse me, Detective?"

"Yes, Ms. Hawkins?"

"I was thinking. I was here last night, and know what the room looked like when I left it. Should I come in and tell you if there is something unusual about the scene?" *Besides a dead body, of course.* She wasn't sure if she wanted him to take up her offer, but the executive meeting center was her responsibility and Mrs. Rudy was her client.

The detective stared at her for what seemed like a solid minute, but was probably only five or six seconds. She struggled to meet his steady gaze, then took a deep breath when he nodded.

Katie tried to hold that breath as she approached the stage. The raised platform held a head table with four chairs and a central podium. It was draped with white tablecloths and gold skirting rented especially for this particular meeting. Mrs. Rudy had insisted upon it; she felt the gold added a distinguished touch.

The body, or Mr. Rudy, Katie quickly corrected herself, was lying face down in the middle aisle directly in front of the podium.

From the direction he was facing, he must have fallen off the stage. She carefully avoided the pool of vomit and other bodily fluids and climbed the stairs on the stage's side.

Nothing looked out of place on the table, so she turned toward the podium. And stared in surprise.

Wertz jumped directly up on the stage. "What's wrong?"

She gazed into his eyes, blue as the Mediterranean Sea, and almost forgot what had bothered her. When she came to her senses, she turned back to the podium and pointed. "It's the mike."

"Don't touch it," he admonished.

"I wasn't going to touch it. But it's odd. See, we label our microphones, so that we can keep track of everything and to make sure that outside rental companies don't take our stuff."

"Did you use a rental company this time?"

She shook her head. "Not for any AV equipment. Just for the skirts."

"Skirts?"

She picked at the fabric wrapped around the base of the table, then remembered she wasn't supposed to be touching anything. "Skirts. But in case you were wondering, they didn't deliver these yesterday. We had them three days ago and Bobby set the tables up himself last night."

"Last night?"

"Yes, last night he worked late setting up the room. We had another group that left at five, so he had to change the setup for Mrs. Rudy's organization."

"And was Mrs. Rudy here as well?" Wertz asked.

"Yes, she was. As was I, until about eight."

"You worked until eight and then came back at 5:45 this morning?"

"You don't keep nine-to-five hours in this job. You probably understand that." She glanced over, pleased when he smiled.

"Perfectly."

"Anyway, Bobby worked until about eleven, then would have come back at six a.m. But, well, I guess he ended up spending the night. He can't have been comfortable, tied up all night."

"Probably not." He nodded his head in agreement then turned back to the scene. "So what's up with the microphone?"

"It's broken," she said simply.

He tilted his head. "And you know this how?"

"Because the last AV report listed that microphone number six was broken. It's been in storage in the AV closet and isn't being used." She waited to see if the detective would react to that revelation, but he was fixated on the trash can under the podium.

He called over one of the crime-scene techs to inspect the trash. The tech reached in with tongs and picked up two thick latex gloves.

Katie considered the gloves and shook her head. "That's not good."

The detective moved past her to take a closer look. "What's not good?"

"We learned in first aid class—all managers have to take the training yearly—anyway, we learned how to safely take off medical gloves. You know, where you partially remove one glove with the other gloved hand, then carefully use it to remove the remaining glove."

Detective Wertz looked at the gloves, then back at her. "And?"

"Paul, the EMT who teaches the course, would flunk whoever took *those* gloves off. Look. That one glove is inside out. That means whoever took it off would have touched the outside of the other glove with his bare skin. That's a good way to contaminate your skin with bodily fluids."

The detective glanced at the gloves, then over at the body, before turning back to her with a satisfied smile. "Bodily fluids, and maybe something much worse than that."

"Like what?" she asked.

He shook his head. "Let's just wait for the medical examiner."

* * * *

Katie spent the rest of the morning tracking down an alternative meeting space for Mrs. Rudy's event. The woman was impossible. Katie couldn't believe she hadn't chosen to reschedule.

She spent the rest of the week wondering if the detectives had managed to figure out who had killed Mr. Rudy. Occasionally, she'd wonder if her client had done the deed. Ha! It was easier to picture someone wanting to kill Mrs. Rudy rather than her husband.

* * * *

On the Friday following the murder, Katie was overseeing the last of the clean-up crew who were steam-cleaning the carpets in the ballroom. Although they managed to remove all traces of poor Mr. Rudy, she didn't think she'd ever forget anything about the event.

Including Detective Wertz. She shook her head as her mind drifted—as it often did—to the handsome police officer. And speak of the devil, she thought, as the man himself strode through the door. She left the cleaners to their task and rushed over to him.

"Is everything okay?" she asked. "We got the approval to clean up yesterday, and we need the ballroom for a wedding this weekend. I hope—"

He raised a hand to stop her. "Everything is fine, Ms. Hawkins. I just, well, I wanted to let you know how it worked out and to thank you for your help."

"*My* help?"

"Well, you provided the most important clue."

Blinking in surprise, she tried to remember what she had said or done. "I did?"

"I had already noted how the victim had died, so I suspected poison. I was trying to figure out who might have wanted to poison Mr. Rudy."

Katie immediately thought of her client. She wondered if the detective was going to tell her that Glenda Rudy was on her way to central booking and a fitting for an orange jumpsuit.

"But when you mentioned the fact about the gloves and that they hadn't been taken off properly, it made me view the scene in a totally different way. That and the fact that you said that the microphone was broken, and that your staff would have known that."

Katie frowned. Even with all the medical and crime shows she watched, she suspected she was missing something. "So?"

"So, I don't think someone was trying to poison Mr. Rudy." Wertz paused dramatically. "I think Mr. Rudy was trying to poison someone else."

She sucked in a breath. "Mrs. Rudy!"

"Bingo! She admitted the divorce was going very poorly, especially for her husband. She was about to get a huge settlement."

Katie shook her head. "So he tried to kill *her*. He knocked out Bobby, stole a microphone, put poison on it." She stopped and waited to see if they had determined the poison already.

"Ricin. Nasty stuff. Made from castor beans, which also happen to be used in leather making."

Katie nodded, remembering that Mr. Rudy was a leather artist. "So he put poison on the microphone, knowing that Mrs. Rudy would be using the microphone first. But when he took off the gloves..."

"He got the ricin on himself," Wertz continued. "And since he'd added some DMSO solvent to the mix, it was quickly absorbed in the skin."

She shook her head. "So Mr. Rudy poisoned himself."

"Looks that way. The medical examiner agrees, based on the residue on the gloves and on the victim's hands. Right where there'd be residue if you took the gloves off incorrectly." He smiled down at her. "So, like I said, you provided the important clue."

She felt herself blush at his compliment. "Did you tell Mrs. Rudy?"

"I just did. Can't say she was terribly grateful. There's a chance this could affect the settlement from the life insurance company since the victim was committing a crime at the time of his death."

"The woman almost gets killed and she's worried about life insurance? She should be relieved she avoided being poisoned." Katie shook her head. She supposed it was as good as they were going to get: a killer brought to justice, the case solved and closed. Too bad the victim in this case wasn't terribly innocent or his intended victim terribly grateful. She shrugged. Not all murder mysteries had happy endings.

Wertz grinned. "Well, let me just say that I'm grateful you figured the bit out about the gloves. And I was wondering if it would be okay if I call you some time. When I'm off-duty, of course."

Katie smiled as she handed over her business card. Now *that* was a happy ending.

Cathy Wiley achieved her lifetime goal of being an author with the publication of *Dead to Writes*, the first in the Cassandra Ellis mysteries. The second novel, *Two Wrongs Don't Make a Write*, continues the series and her dream. She draws upon her experience in the hospitality business to show the lighter, quirkier side of people, and upon her own morbid mind to show the darker side. In her free time, she enjoys scuba diving, dancing, wine, food, and reading. She lives near Baltimore, Maryland, with two very spoiled cats.

MEAN GIRLS
by Donna Andrews

"Where the hell *were* you Friday?" Tiffany shrieked as I walked through the office door.

I ignored her and continued to my desk.

"Now, now," Jessica said. "Let's try to behave like adults. Kate," she said, turning to me, "we're very disappointed in you. You were supposed to open the office and cover the phones on the day after Thanksgiving. Hasn't Dr. Grace already spoken to you about the importance of keeping your commitments?"

For Jessica, apparently, behaving like an adult meant adopting the kind of tone you'd use when talking to a four-year-old child. I set down my purse and took off my coat.

"There's just no use talking to some people," Amanda said, while staring at the top of the window behind me. In the eight months I'd been working for Edith Grace Personnel Services, she had yet to look me in the face or address me directly.

All three of the mean girls, as I called them, were lined up in front of my desk. Normally, they waited until afternoon to pick on me. Maybe they'd missed doing it over the four-day Thanksgiving weekend.

Maybe this would be the day they'd push too far and propel me into quitting this thankless, dead-end job.

Or maybe I wouldn't have to quit. Business was slow, and it was an open secret that Dr. Grace would probably be downsizing her staff before too long. A sane boss would fire one of the mean girls, who were overpaid, underworked, and largely interchangeable. Tiffany and Amanda were slightly ruder, but Jessica, though arguably incompetent, was better at sucking up to the boss. And they were all expert at blaming anything that went wrong on me. So the odds were that Dr. Grace would lay me off instead. As I stared at the frowning faces in front of me, I almost hoped she would.

"Good morning to you, too." I tried to keep my tone even and my face cheerful. "What seems to be the problem?"

They all three blinked and gawked at me for a few seconds.

"You didn't come to the office on Friday," Tiffany said.

"Yes, I did," I said. "Unfortunately, I wasn't able to get *in* the office because the key I was given didn't open the outer door."

I reached into my purse and pulled out the key in question, still attached to a small tag marked "Building Entrance" in our boss's spidery handwriting.

"That's impossible," Jessica said. "That's the key we've always used."

"Oh, dear," Tiffany said. "Didn't we change the lock after the last receptionist left?"

Jessica's mouth formed a little O. Amanda sighed loudly. Tiffany actually growled. I had to suppress a giggle at this rare break in the mean girls' solidarity.

Jessica recovered her composure and turned to me, a frown marring her perfectly made-up face.

"Still, you could have *called* someone," she said.

"I called Dr. Grace and left a message," I said. "I knew the three of you were planning to be out of town. So after waiting outside the building in the freezing cold for an hour, I went home. I kept my cell phone with me for the rest of the day, but Dr. Grace never returned my call."

I refrained from adding, "So there!" They could probably hear it in my voice.

"Let's just see about that, shall we?" Jessica said. "I can't imagine that Dr. Grace would not have done something if she actually got such a message."

She set off briskly down the hall toward Dr. Grace's office.

"Someone slipped a nasty note under the front door," Tiffany said. "And who knows how many other clients went away upset." She was waving a slip of paper—the nasty note, I assumed. But her eyes were on my in-box. In fact, she and Amanda were both staring at the foot-high stack of work the three of them had dumped on my desk Wednesday, when they heard Dr. Grace order me to come in on

Friday. I wondered how many of the projects in that stack they were supposed to have finished by this morning?

"Unbelievable," Amanda said to the ceiling. "Come on, Tiff."

They followed Jessica down the hall. I sat down and pressed a key to wake up my computer.

"Dr. Grace?" I heard Jessica saying, as she knocked on our boss's door. "Can we talk to you for a moment?"

Dr. Grace would probably look puzzled and disappointed, and claim that she didn't recall getting my message, and ask if I was quite sure I had dialed her number correctly. At least that's what she'd done a month ago when I'd called her to say I'd had a flat tire on my way to work. So this time I'd followed up my voice mail message with an email from my home computer.

"Dr. Grace? Are you in there?"

Of course she was in there. It was only a few minutes until the regular nine a.m. Monday staff meeting. Any second now she would emerge, ready to pontificate to her minions and receive their daily tributes of candy, baked goods, lattes, and flowers.

I scanned my own email. Yes, there were several complaints from people who'd tried to reach us Friday. And the copy of my Friday message. Any reasonable person would understand what had happened.

And if they were unreasonable and fired me, maybe that wouldn't be the worst thing in the world. Maybe—

"Oh, my God!" Jessica exclaimed from the other end of the hallway.

Someone began shrieking, but I couldn't tell who it was until Tiffany burst into the reception area, still shrieking.

"What now?" I muttered.

Jessica dashed in behind Tiffany.

"Now, Tiffany," she was saying. "We must be brave."

Tiffany threw herself onto the couch in the waiting area and added sobs to her shrieks.

"Go help Amanda!" Jessica snapped at me.

I got up and headed down the hall. I found Amanda crumpled in the doorway of Dr. Grace's office. Her eyelids were fluttering, so either she'd fainted and was coming around or she was faking it and vexed that no one had come to her aid.

I stepped over Amanda and looked to see what the problem was. "Damn," I said.

Dr. Grace was slumped over her desk, arms outstretched as if she had attempted a swan dive onto its polished mahogany surface. An uncomfortable-looking position, but one that gave me a good view of the knife stuck in her back.

I pulled out my cell phone and punched 911.

The first uniformed officer showed up in less than five minutes. He was followed by more uniformed officers. Then a couple of EMTs who seemed a bit annoyed at being called out for someone so clearly past saving. A pair of detectives flashing gold badges. And then a small swarm of crime-scene technicians.

The mean girls and I got to watch all this from the glass-walled conference room off the reception area, under the watchful eyes of a uniformed officer who made sure we didn't talk to one another. The mean girls sniffled and looked shell-shocked. I had to remind myself that humming "Ding, Dong, the Witch Is Dead!" would probably not be a wise move.

The room was already set up for the usual Monday morning staff meeting. The mean girls all stayed at the far end of the room, away from the chair where, if she hadn't been murdered, Dr. Grace would have been presiding. I wasn't ever invited to their meetings, of course, but I would watch the whole show through the glass walls.

I wouldn't have hesitated to sit in Dr. Grace's chair—in fact, I'd have enjoyed annoying them by doing so—but I could get a better view of what the police were doing from the middle of the table.

After a great long while, one of the detectives stepped into the room.

"Which one of you is Ms. Malone?" he asked.

"Me." I raised my hand as if in class. The mean girls all flashed triumphant, malicious little smiles at each other.

"You're the one who called 911?" he asked.

I nodded.

"Great," he said. "I'd like to start with you."

Three pairs of hostile eyes followed me out.

The detective led me into the one empty office and sat behind the desk. As I sat down, I glanced through the glass walls of the office. In the conference room, the mean girls were sitting in a cluster, watching me. My stomach tightened. After all, everyone knew how I felt about Dr. Grace. What if the whole key fiasco hadn't been an accident—what if it was part of some convoluted plot by one of the mean girls to knock off Dr. Grace and frame me?

Of course, that would take brains. Not something the mean girls had a surplus of.

I'd expected the detective to demand where I was on the day after Thanksgiving, but he started out in a more casual tone.

"So," he began. "Just what is Edith Grace Personnel Services?"

"Sort of a specialized human resources company," I said. "If a company's downsizing and doesn't want their own HR people to go through the trauma of breaking the news to the victims, they hire EGPS."

"So you fire people for a living?"

"Me? No, I just type and answer the phone and mind the reception desk. Dr. Grace and the mean girls do the firing."

"Mean girls?" He raised one eyebrow.

Oops. "That's what I call them. Jessica, Amanda, and Tiffany. Mean girls. Because that's how they behave."

The corner of his mouth twitched slightly, as if he were trying not to smile. Then he gave in and chuckled.

"My sister used to come home from high school complaining about what the mean girls had done to her that day," he said. "Been a while since I've heard the phrase."

"Maybe some of those high-school mean girls grow up to be pleasant women," I said. "Not these three. They're perfect for the job."

"For firing people?"

I nodded.

"Don't they also help people find new jobs?"

"Not exactly," I said. "They do outplacement services. Classes on resume writing and how to find job leads and present yourself well in an interview. Actually getting a job's your own problem."

"You sound a little cynical about what your company does."

"Not my company," I said. "I'm just working here until I find a job in my field."

"And that is?"

"I was a reporter." I wondered if he knew how moribund the newspaper industry was, how many dozens of applicants there were for every job that came open, and how very likely I was to spend the next couple of decades working thankless jobs like this one.

But not with Dr. Grace. Or the mean girls. The thought cheered me up.

"You don't look as upset as the others," he said.

"I've only been here eight months," I said. "It hasn't been a ball of fun."

"You disliked Dr. Grace, then?"

"Yes." I didn't see any reason to lie. "Not enough to kill her, of course. And I suppose at the very least I should be upset that I'll be losing my job."

"You don't think they'll keep you on?" he asked. "Surely without Dr. Grace the company will need all the help they can get."

"I doubt if the company will survive without Dr. Grace," I said. "She's the one who has the credentials and the contacts. Had, that is. All they know how to do is fire people."

"Tough job," he said.

Tougher on the ones getting fired if you asked me. Should I tell him how much the mean girls seemed to enjoy it? How they put on their sad, sympathetic faces as easily as pulling on a sweater, and then at the end of the day gathered in the coffee room to make fun of their poor clients.

"I wouldn't want to do it," I said aloud.

"So if you or any of her employees murdered Dr. Grace, you'd be killing the goose that lays the golden eggs," he said.

"Only copper eggs in my case. But yes."

"You must have a lot of disgruntled people coming through this office."

"Yeah," I said. "But wouldn't most of them be more disgruntled at the companies who fired them?" I was happier when I thought he was suspicious of the mean girls. Was it my long-dormant reporter's instincts that told me one of the mean girls had to have done it? Or was it just that I hoped he'd find one of them guilty?

"Still," he went on. "Maybe one of those disgruntled unemployed people focused his anger at Dr. Grace. Can you remember anyone in particular?"

So for the next hour, he picked my brains about disgruntled clients. Were any of them more disgruntled than usual? Had we received threats? Did Dr. Grace have enemies? Did all the mean girls like her? And what had I been doing over the last four days? I was relieved that I did have an alibi of sorts for the time I was at the office on Friday, even if it was only the homeless man who slept on the steps of the church across the street. Good thing I'd turned down his offer to get me into the building by breaking a window.

"So who do you think did it?" the detective finally asked.

"One of the mean girls," I said. "No idea which."

He nodded. His face didn't give away much. I had no idea if he thought I was a reliable witness or a suspiciously disgruntled employee.

Then one of the uniformed officers escorted me back to the conference room, and I waited while the detective interviewed the mean girls, one by one. For a while I watched the activity outside as police officers and technicians came and went. But eventually that died down, so I pulled a paperback out of my purse and read, ignoring the glares of the others.

Finally Amanda came back into the room, still leaking tears, followed by the detective.

"I want to thank all of you for your time," he said.

He looked irritated. I would, too, after spending a couple of hours with my co-workers.

Or maybe he was just hungry. My stomach picked that moment to growl loudly. The mean girls all glared at me, as if I'd done it deliberately to mar this solemn occasion.

"This is still an open investigation," the detective went on. "And I will probably have more questions for all of you."

But it looked as if he was letting us go for now. Good. I wished he'd hurry. As the detective handed out his cards and asked us to stay in the area, I found myself eyeing the two muffins still sitting on a small china plate at what would have been Dr. Grace's place at the table. Part of the usual weekly tribute. The muffins were low-fat, sugar-free bran muffins—I'd once tasted a leftover one and found it about as appetizing as sawdust. But as hungry as I was, even the muffins were starting to look good.

Wait a minute. The muffins were there as usual. Beside them, also as usual, was the vase of fresh flowers that would grace the table during their meeting and Dr. Grace's desk for the rest of the day. But something was missing.

"Where's the latte?" I said aloud.

Everyone turned to look at me.

"What's that?" the detective asked.

"Where's Dr. Grace's latte?" I asked. "Every morning Tiffany brings her a bran muffin from the organic bakery down the street. Amanda brings her fresh flowers from the stand by the Metro stop. Sometimes candy, if she can get to the Godiva store, but usually flowers. And Jessica always stops at Starbucks to bring her a low-fat, sugar-free latte with skim milk. Where's the latte?"

Jessica's face was fun to watch as it changed from annoyance to surprise to utter horror as she thought through what I'd just said. And like the rest of us, she was staring at the tall brown Starbucks paper cup in front of her own place at the table.

"Dr. Grace didn't…I mean, knew she probably wouldn't…"

Then she shut up. She didn't actually say "I want my attorney," but I had the feeling those words were in her future.

She looked at Tiffany and Amanda, as if pleading for support.

They both hitched their chairs away from her. Tiffany hitched hers so far she was sitting next to me.

"We knew Dr. Grace was thinking of letting someone go," Tiffany told the detective. "But we thought it was—I mean, I suppose we should have realized it would have to be Jessica."

"Some people truly are impossible, aren't they?" Amanda said. She glanced at me briefly with a faint smile before turning to stare at a spot a foot above Jessica's head.

Maybe in high school I'd have been tempted. But even in high school, I don't think I'd have fallen for their overtures. I ignored them, and stood up.

"Can I still leave?" I asked the detective. "And is it okay for me to clean out my desk right now? I'm resigning, effective immediately, and I'd rather not have to come back to this snake pit."

"Be my guest," he said.

Tiffany and Amanda both rose, uttering feeble bleats of protest.

"Ladies," the detective said. "I have a few more questions for all three of you."

They sat back down again, looking forlorn. The detective led Jessica back to the office he'd been using as his interview room.

Packing wouldn't take long. By the time he finished with the mean girls and hauled Jessica down to the station, I'd be long gone. Maybe I'd stop on the way home and buy some champagne to celebrate my freedom.

Better yet, maybe I'd stop at Starbucks and toast my victory with a latte.

Donna Andrews was born in Yorktown, Virginia, and now lives in Reston, Virginia. *The Real Macaw*, (July 2011, Minotaur), is the latest book in her Agatha- and Anthony-winning Meg Langslow series, and *Some Like It Hawk* will be released in July 2012. She has also written four books in the Turing Hopper series from Berkley Prime Crime. For more information: http://donnaandrews.com.

WHEN DUTY CALLS
by Art Taylor

Keri is just setting out the silverware when the Colonel calls across from the living room with a new question. He's watching the Military Channel and finishing up the cocktail she made for him—a thimble of Virginia Gentleman, a generous portion of soda, another light splash of whiskey on top to make it smell like a stronger drink. The Colonel's house has an open floor plan from the kitchen through the dining room to where he sits, and as she's finished up dinner, she's listened to him arguing lightly with the program's depiction of Heartbreak Ridge, reminiscing about his own stint in Korea, rambling in his own way. "Last rally of the Shermans," he mused aloud, and something about "optics" and "maneuverability" and then—a different tone than Keri's heard in the four months she's known him—"Is the perimeter secure, Sergeant?"

"The perimeter?" Keri asks, cautiously. She's grown used to these sudden shifts in subject—learned quickly just to roll along with the conversation, even in the first days after she and Pete moved in. But she still stumbles sometimes to catch up and find the right response.

The Colonel turns in his chair—turning *on* her, Keri thinks, expecting his regular confusion or the occasional rebuke—but he doesn't look her way. He's listening, it seems, his jaw fixed, his chin jutting more than usual. The tendons in his frail arms tighten, his tie tugs at the skin around his neck, his whole body perches alert, if unsteadily so. Medals and photos crowd the wall behind him. Round stickers dot many of them and almost everything else in the living room: lamps, books, bookcases, the chair itself. Red, white, and blue.

"Incoming," he says.

"No one's out there, Colonel," she tries to reassure him. Not anymore, at least, since that pair of surveyors out in the woods had packed up their bags a half-hour before, one of them waving at her through the window before cranking up, heading out. They'd stayed late. She was glad to see them go.

"Vibrations," the Colonel whispers. "A good soldier can sense these things. Life and death." Just his mind wandering, she knows, just another bout of dementia, but for a moment the seriousness of his tone, the weight of his words, stop her. Despite herself, she looks toward the door. Has he actually heard something? The surveyors had forgotten something, returned unannounced. Or maybe Pete had canceled his Tuesday night classes in town to come home early. But no. There's no knock at the door, and no sound of a key turning in it. No muddy shoes being brushed against the mat. No sound of tires on the gravel drive. Just the TV program rolling on. Strategies, skirmishes, victories, defeat.

"Did Pete call?" she asks.

"Negative," the Colonel says casually, just the hint of disdain, and then he relaxes, settles back into his chair. "Radio silence has been maintained."

There's something melancholy in his answer, or maybe it's Keri's imagination this time. She wonders if he even notices how seldom the phone rings—for either of them. Calls come so rarely that she once raised the receiver to her ear just to make sure there was a dial tone there. More than once, actually.

"Lasagna's ready," she tells him, and the Colonel brightens up.

"Officer's Club," he says eagerly. Date night, she knows.

Other nights, mealtime is just "chow," but on Tuesdays Pete always stays on campus late, and the Colonel seems to love those nights best. She's not sure how she goes from being his staff sergeant to being his...wife? Girlfriend? Daughter? She's not sure about that either: which role she plays. He doesn't seem to know who she is at all, has never even spoken her name. But sometimes when Pete is out of the way, the Colonel reaches over and presses his gnarled fingers over her hand, pats, squeezes, breaking Keri's heart a little each time.

* * * *

"It's a good deal," Pete said after the interview with the Colonel's daughter, after she'd offered them the job. Do a little housecleaning, make a couple of meals a day for the old man, and in exchange: free rent, a grocery stipend, a monthly bonus. A six-month stint. "The whole semester," Pete went on. "Not just a good deal, but a *great* one, especially with teaching assistant stipends these days." He didn't need to add that Keri was unemployed herself, had been for a while.

It was that last part that convinced Keri and kept her from pointing out how much of the cooking and housecleaning quickly fell to her. Pete was at least pulling his weight elsewhere, wasn't he? Teaching a freshman survey course in western drama? Pursuing his own PhD? She could hardly complain about doing the dishes when he had lessons to prep and essays to grade and all that reading to do: Shakespeare, Ibsen, O'Neill, Beckett, Miller. And then fitting in work on his doctoral dissertation around the edges. He was already the golden boy of the doctoral program, destined to be the star of some big English department. She shared those dreams, and she tried not to nag him about her own. That wasn't the woman she wanted to be—about work or marriage, about children somewhere down the line.

"We're both in school," Pete had said more than once when she talked about the future. "Student loans won't pay themselves." And that dissertation wouldn't write itself. And tenure-line jobs didn't come knocking on your door. School first, life later. She'd grown accustomed to that.

But now, with the semester living at the Colonel's, with the savings, he'd hinted more about next steps. "With the money we're saving here, we can set aside a little bit," he said, "for the future."

Maybe it was for the best for her to shoulder the work at the house while he focused on his education. And maybe there were other good reasons that Pete's duties around the house were more limited. After all, the Colonel didn't seem entirely to approve of him. He didn't like the meals that Pete tried to make ("too spicy" once, "too bland" another time), he didn't like all the time he spent reading ("needs to get off his duff"), and he generally peppered Pete with complaints on a regular basis.

"A trip to the barber in your future anytime, son?" the Colonel asked one morning. "That hardly seems regulation length."

Other mornings—more than once: "Those shoes need a good buffing, soldier."

And on the nights when Pete did join them for dinner: "Where's your tie, boy?"

The Colonel wears a tie each night for dinner, tied in an elaborate knot. "A Full Windsor," he told Keri when she asked. "Most men employ the Half-Windsor or the Four-in-Hand, but that's too casual for me."

"A little old school, don't you think?" Pete said, when Keri asked him to try it one evening, just a single meal, just to humor the old man. "And that wasn't part of the deal, now, was it?"

"Recruits these days," the Colonel sometimes says, just under his breath. "A sorry lot, all of them."

* * * *

When Keri stands up to clear the table, the Colonel stands quickly as well to help. Even when she dismisses him—"No worries, I can do it" (he's dropped plates before)—he hesitates before heading back toward the TV. He's waiting for her, she knows.

"Just let me get this cleaned up," she says, "and I'll be right in, okay?"

"Roger that," he says. "Rendezvous..." He glances at his watch. "Twenty hundred hours?"

"Roger," Keri salutes, mock-serious. These days, she doesn't have to count out the real time anymore. "I'll meet you in the den."

She stores the lasagna away in squares—leftovers for the week ahead—and sets aside a large slice for Pete, though she knows he'll already have eaten dinner and probably gone out for drinks after class. Winding-down time after the intensity of the three-hour seminars, he's explained.

The window above the kitchen sink has a wide view of the yard. The gravel driveway stretches off to the right between the trees, a hundred yards to the main road, a lonely stretch leading "off base." Shadows play in the woods directly ahead, thick with oak and pine and beech, many of them now tied with red ribbons, marked for timber. Moonlight glistens on the lake off to the left, just barely in sight from this vantage, a rough shoreline that Keri and the Colonel have walked on more than one afternoon, counting Canada geese. A full moon tonight, Keri notes, as if that might explain the tension in the air.

Throughout dinner, the Colonel seemed restless, attentive. Now, as Keri scrubs at the casserole pan, she finds herself watchful, too. Is there "incoming"? She thinks about the people that she's seen in and around the property sometimes. Fishermen bring small skiffs close to shore or actually trudge down the driveway in their waders, tossing a small wave toward the house as they pass. Hunters often wander through the woods, unsure whose property they've crossed into at any point. More than once, teenagers have pulled a car up the drive—couples, groups, looking for a place to hook up, get high, get into trouble. Then, beginning last week, came the onslaught of real estate agents and surveyors, the men from the tree service, the crew taking soil samples, the beginning of the end. Today's surveyors had lingered until almost dusk, and she'd had the feeling of being trapped somehow, or watched at least, like she and the Colonel were on display, sad curiosities. A couple of times, she caught the men just standing there, smoking cigarettes, staring toward the house. Leering, she thought, no better than construction workers, ogling passersby.

She doesn't know which is worse—the isolation she'd been feeling out here or these sudden intrusions, and the knowledge of what it means. Stuck somewhere between the two and spurred on by the Colonel's own brewing vigilance tonight, her imagination leaps ahead again, playing tricks on her. Is that the red tip of a cigarette butt? No, just one of the ribbons flapping in the moonlight. Did that shadow move? No, just a branch swaying in the breeze.

"Full moon," she says aloud, and then remembers her horoscope from earlier that day: *Surprises abound. Follow where the evening takes you. All will become clear.* Pete still makes fun of her for reading them each morning.

Behind her, the Colonel turns up the TV—hinting for her to join him. The announcer is talking about the Trojan War, the horse that made history, the importance of surprise. Keri shivers a little.

"Coming," she calls to him.

The pan still isn't clean. And she hasn't even started on the knife, crusted with cheese. She leaves both to soak until later—even till tomorrow perhaps.

* * * *

"He's dotty," Margaret, the former caretaker, had said, the second time they'd met—the passing on of the keys. She was an older woman: fifties, stout, frizzy-haired. "You'll find out soon enough. And you've got your work cut out for you with him. With all of them."

The first time they'd met was when Keri and Pete had been interviewed for the job. Margaret had brooded along the edges of the conversation as Claire, the youngest of the Colonel's children, put a different spin on the situation: "The world has passed my father by," she said. "We've striven to preserve his old glories, revere his achievements." She swept an arm about the room. Medals and honors dominated one wall. Photographs with politicians and military leaders lined another, many of them long dead, Keri had since learned. Several framed boxes held guns, relics of a recent past, like museum pieces but brimming with menace. "Unfortunately, everything that my father trained for, everything that he lived for—none of it has much purpose here."

Claire explained that it was just short-term. Margaret had been called to help her own father; plans were already afoot to sell the property, but might take some time; and they were finally looking into "more professional care" for the Colonel—a step they'd dreaded and delayed for too long. Claire herself had tended to him for several years after her mother died. "But I couldn't manage any longer," she explained. "Physically, yes, but emotionally... Well, watching someone you love so dearly deteriorate, become a shadow, sometimes you just feel yourself breaking down as well." Keri and Pete were a stopgap. She was sure they understood.

The Colonel was napping while they talked. Margaret had shot a couple of looks at Keri throughout the conversation: envy, disbelief, warning glares? Keri hadn't been sure. (Margaret told her later, on the sly, that Claire was a drinker. Claire, in turn, confided that Margaret was a thief—little things, but hardly negligible.)

It was after the Colonel went down for his nap another afternoon, only a week ago now, that Claire and her siblings—Beatrice and Dwight—had made their inventory. This was the first time that Keri had met the other two, since both lived just out of state, and Margaret's comment about having her work cut out for her with "all of them" echoed throughout the day.

With Pete on campus again—early office hours, eternal office hours—Keri had played host alone. Claire asked her to make a salad for lunch, "something simple, no trouble," and Keri had, laying it out on the table, not planning to join them until the Colonel insisted, asking his son to move down a seat, make room for the ladies.

Dwight had smirked at that. "Aye aye, sir," he said, taking his salad with him as he slid down.

The Colonel had seemed to recognize them only dimly, but he nodded politely when Beatrice spoke about her children's latest report cards and Dwight talked about the business finally turning a profit again last quarter—"despite what the president's doing," he insisted, which prompted Beatrice to complain bitterly about the state of political discourse in the country today. More smirks from Dwight at that, and cold looks from Claire.

The Colonel had watched all of them with interest but no reaction. Claire tried at each turn of the conversation to nudge her father to recall Beatrice's children or the nature of Dwight's business or just the name of that current president, but she had finally given up, simply watching the Colonel with a mixture of curiosity and distress. Keri had watched each of them and didn't know exactly how she felt.

After lunch was done and the Colonel had retired to his room for some light R&R, the three of them began to divvy up the belongings, prepping to make an easy sweep of it between the day they moved the old man out and the scheduled demolition of the house, quick work for the condo development ahead. Claire had brought small circular stickers to help with the division. Each of them would simply mark the items they wanted to take. "Pop will appreciate the patriotic touch," Dwight said, holding up a package of red stickers and leaving blue and white for his sisters. Unmarked items would be slated for donation to the Salvation Army. "And a military nod again," Dwight said, already beginning to stake down his claims.

When the three of them ended up squabbling about an autographed photo of Eisenhower standing with the Colonel and his late wife, Keri felt like she saw the three of them most clearly. Beatrice, the eldest, argued that the photo was hers because she was actually in the picture, cradled in their mother's arms. Dwight, now the baby of the bunch, pointed out that he'd been named after the president, "which ought to give me dibs." Meanwhile Claire—caretaker-turned-peacemaker—tried as best she could to keep the simmer from becoming a boil.

"So doesn't that give you claim to all of this, Bea?" Dwight demanded. "You saw it first, you were there first? It's all yours?" And then trying to recruit Claire to the cause: "Isn't that how it's always been?"

"That's not what I'm saying," Beatrice said. "I'm saying I'm *in* the damn picture. It's a picture of *me*."

"Let's leave it for father, for his room at the nursing home," Claire said. "He always loved it so."

"He wouldn't even know it's there," Dwight said.

"Let's leave it unmarked then," Claire went on. "No one will take it. We can donate it somewhere. A tribute that—"

"Stick it up in some museum?" Dwight said. "Hell no. That sucker's *worth* something."

"Is that what you're planning?" Beatrice flashed with rage. "Selling it somewhere?"

"Please keep your voices down," Claire said, and Keri could sense something stretched thin in her own voice. "He'll hear us."

"If he does wake up," Dwight told Keri, "just keep him in the room for a while."

"How should I do that?" Keri asked, startled by the sound of her own voice.

"Tell him," Dwight began. "Tell him the base is on lockdown." He seemed to be thinking. He grinned broadly, something cruel behind it. "There's a sniper. Delta Force is handling it. Tell him, 'Orders from the general.'"

"General." Beatrice snorted. "Is that how you picture yourself in all this?"

Bickering spun out of selfishness, anger where there should have been empathy, lies built high on the Colonel's dementia—Keri hated it all.

But later, she reflected that she wasn't much better, at least in one regard.

When the real estate agents, surveyors, and repairmen had made their rounds, Keri had dutifully pretended to the Colonel that they were visiting dignitaries, military attaches, envoys from D.C. And when the Colonel woke from his nap and asked what all the dots were for—on the lamps, on the furniture, everywhere—Keri told him "inventory" and then "supply room," trying to think of the right term, build another lie he might believe.

"Midnight requisitions," the Colonel said vaguely, with a sigh of contempt, and something about a "five-fingered discount," and then, grinning himself, just like Dwight had, "Oh, well, Sergeant, we'll just have to requisition it all back," like he knew the game.

* * * *

"Lear," Pete said when Keri told him all about it. "The grasping, the selfishness. Siblings showing their true colors. Claire sounds like the best of them: 'You have brought me up and loved me, and I return you those duties back as are right and fit, obey you, love you, and most honor you.'" Pete performed the last part with a stagy British lilt.

"It didn't feel like honor," Keri said. "Or love either."

"That's what Lear thought, too." Pete raised his eyebrow. "And you know how that turned out. So who got the photo?"

"Beatrice," Keri said. "She traded Dwight the dining room table for it, but he said it didn't matter, he'd get it back someday. Told her that since she was older, she'd go first. 'I'll keep these handy,' he said, and he waved his extra stickers in the air."

"Charming," Pete said. "Sorry I missed it." Keri had hoped for a little more empathy, but Pete was already moving on: "You know, I think I'll add *Lear* to the syllabus. Sub it in instead of *Othello*—that's done too much in high school anyway, don't you think? And *Lear*—"

"But what should *we* do?" Keri insisted. "What's *our* role in all this?"

She doesn't entirely remember his answer—several possibilities, comparing them to the Earl of Kent or the Fool. Did Keri have a touch of Cordelia herself? Little of substance, nothing practical, no solace. Instead, it's more of Margaret's words that have persisted: "Not a word of thanks, unless you demand it. Not a single token of appreciation, unless you take it yourself. I'm telling you: You've already been bought and paid for."

* * * *

The Colonel dresses and undresses himself, handles all of his own bathroom duties, but Keri follows up with him each morning and each night. This evening, as usual, he's had trouble with his nightclothes—his "old man jammies," Pete calls them. One side of his top hangs low, unfastened, while the skipped button bunches out on the other side, the fabric opening to reveal the aged flesh of his belly, a thin tangle of gray hairs. "He does it on purpose," Pete has joked, "just so you can fluff him up." She tries not to think about that as she straightens the buttoning, a complicated dance of discretion and helpfulness.

The Colonel always apologizes to one version or another of who he thinks she is. "Aging is an indignity, Sergeant," he's said before. And other times: "In all our many years together, my darling, did you ever believe it would come to this?" These seem his only flashes of awareness about time and his place in it, but even those moments are dim with confusion.

"I've not been a good husband, dear," he tells her tonight. "A good father, either, to—" He stops, he catches himself. Some small reality intrudes. "Thank you for looking after me," he says. He strokes her cheek.

She puts him to bed, she tucks him in, she turns out his light. Nearly always, he's staring at the ceiling when she leaves him. Tonight, he watches the window.

"The guards," he says. "The duty roster."

"Yes, yes," she tells him, and she closes the door.

Back in her own room, she tries to go to bed, but finds herself restless, irritable, waiting once more for Pete, angry a little at him this time—and even more of each emotion tonight because of whatever's gotten into the Colonel. She lies in the darkness for a while, staring at the shadows playing outside her own window, at that full moon raging, and then she turns on the light once more to read. She wants to keep up with what Pete's doing, give them more to talk about, so she'd been following his syllabus. The class has already reached *Lear*, and she takes down the bulky *Riverside Shakespeare* from the nightstand, reminds herself again to get a more readable copy, then picks up mid-scene where she'd fallen asleep the night before:

> *This is the excellent foppery of the world, that, when we are sick in fortune,—often the surfeit of our own behavior,—we make guilty of our disasters the sun, the moon, and the stars: as if we were villains by necessity; fools by heavenly compulsion; knaves, thieves, and treachers, by spherical predominance; drunkards, liars, and adulterers, by an enforced obedience of planetary influence; and all that we are evil in, by a divine thrusting on: an admirable evasion of whoremaster man, to lay his goatish disposition to the charge of a star!*

It's near the end of the monologue that she hears the click of the front door—opening, closing. Pete at last, sooner than she expected. Sometimes he calls, usually she sees the sweep of his headlights against the window. He's surprising her this time.

She's left a note for him: "A plate of lasagna in the fridge. Microwave two minutes. XO. Me." But she hopes he won't see it, that he'll just come back to her, ease this troubled evening. She listens for his footsteps coming down the hallway, but instead, she hears him trip over something, and she knows then he's been drinking after class, too many drinks again, and suddenly it seems like he'll just complicate the night further instead of improving it.

She starts to go out to him, confront him, but no, she'll wait. She picks up the book again:

Edgar—

[Enter Edgar.]

*and pat! he comes, like the catastrophe of the old comedy. My
cue is villainous melancholy, with a sigh like Tom o' Bedlam.
O, these eclipses do portend these divisions! Fa, sol, la, mi.*

She's stopped by the sound of the front door, opening and closing
once more.

He's gone out again? Keri lays the book down, steps to the
window to see what he's doing. But his car's not out there at all,
the yard looks empty. And then the sound of the front door opening
again, and soon after, the sound of glass breaking, but muffled as if
from a great distance.

Incoming, she thinks, and now her senses tingle, her whole body
as alert as the Colonel's had seemed earlier.

She picks up the bedside phone. She'll call 911. She'll call Pete,
already hurrying him homeward with her mind. But there's no dial
tone, just a dull ominous emptiness on the receiver.

Radio silence, she thinks, and then she remembers the Colonel's
other words. *Life and death.*

And then she just thinks about the Colonel himself.

* * * *

His door is still closed, she sees when she leaves her own room.
There's relief in that, though she recognizes the irony: the old warrior
protected by the defenseless woman. But he would only add confusion on top of whatever danger is out there. And the truth is she's
not entirely defenseless. She's carrying the biggest object in the
bedroom—that complete Shakespeare—though she's unsure whether
it might best work as a weapon or as armor. She shudders to think it
might come to that.

As she eases down the hallway, she wonders who's out there. One
of the leering surveyors, after all? That's why they'd stayed so late
today. They were casing the house, returning now to rob it. Or one
of those college kids who sometimes drove down the wrong road—a
prank this time, a dare, a different kind of trouble. She remembers

too how Claire called Margaret a thief, remembers Margaret's own words that you got no token of thanks unless you took it.

The living room is dark, just as she'd left it, with only the moonlight streaming in from various windows, casting shadows around the room.

Then one of the shadows near the dining room table moves, a silhouette stumbling toward the living room. The dim form lifts a pair of pictures from the wall, returns toward the table, lays the pictures flat. Its arm raises high into the air, some object in its grasp, and smashes down sharply. A crunching sound.

Dwight, she realizes, unsure where the knowledge came from. And then she looks again at the empty spaces dotting the wall, the pictures that the intruder is destroying. The Eisenhower is among the missing photos. Dwight would get it, one way or another. There truly was something evil behind that smirk of his, beneath those callous comments.

Suddenly, the book in her hand doesn't seem protection enough.

The guns on the wall, she thinks. Are any of them loaded? How easily could she break the case? Would she know how to use one? But Dwight would stop her. He stands in the way, still fidgeting with things on the table. He could get to those guns first. In fact, she understands now, he's already taken one of them from its box, hasn't he? One of the gun cases stands empty, its glass front shattered. That's the sound Keri had heard. That's what Dwight is holding over his head, what he brings down once more against the table.

The knife. The one she left soaking in the lasagna pan. She can get to that. It's a clear line into the kitchen. It's not a gun, but it's better than Shakespeare. At least she won't be entirely unarmed.

As soon as she's thought it, she's done it. A quick sprint, and she's at the sink. Hand in soapy water, fingers slipping around the handle. But Dwight has come up behind her, grabbed her arm, pushed her against the counter. Keri can't get a grip on the knife.

Hot breath brushes against her neck, carrying with it the stench of alcohol. "You should've stayed in bed," the voice huffs, a snarl there, an undertone of amusement. But it's a woman's voice. Not Dwight, not at all. "It's just a break-in," the woman slurs quietly. "Vandalism.

You were asleep. You didn't hear, you didn't know." Keri tries to shuffle around, to gain an edge, but the woman holds fast, surprisingly strong. "All those years, year upon year. And they think they have any right here? They never cared about him, not once. They don't deserve any of this." She coos, she soothes: "Just let it happen. You know it's right." And then a dark whisper: "I'll compensate you."

Keri shoves her elbow back into doughy flesh, hears the sharp intake of breath. Freed for a moment, she reaches toward the sink. But there's not enough time. Before Keri can grab the knife, she feels fingers around her throat. "This isn't between you and me," the woman says, a snarl now, and maybe it wasn't their fight, but it is now. The woman's grip is relentless, squeezing, pressing. "They can't know it was me. They can't ever know."

Keri pushes off the counter then, shoving as hard as she can, and the two of them sprawl backward across the room. But the woman hangs on, and then she's on top of Keri, slamming her head against the floor. Keri's pulse throbs grimly, there's a roar in her skull, a pounding, and then an explosion as if her head has burst.

Just as quickly the grip relaxes. The other woman falls away, a thud on the floor beside her.

The lights come on soon after, blinding, and Keri hears the Colonel's voice—a single word, frail and nearly indistinct, pleading, concerned. She rises up from the floor then, and gets her first look at the body sprawled beside her—Claire's body, bleeding heavily from where a bullet has ripped through her torso—and at the damage the woman had done.

Spray paint covers the kitchen cabinets, what looks like teen graffiti, like those young joyriders had not just driven down the road but finally come in. The lampshades have been slashed methodically, and more pictures have been pulled down from the wall. Broken glass is everywhere, shards dotting the carpet. The frame on the Eisenhower is shattered, the picture itself torn. The corner of another photo peeks out from beneath a towel on the kitchen table, one of the antique pistols dropped on top of it.

At the edge of the hallway stands the Colonel, a handgun at his side, this one not an antique. He's wearing his full uniform, every button clasped perfectly, the medals gleaming in the sudden light, his posture perfect.

He speaks softly again—a second word now, perplexed and incredulous where that first word had been pleading—and then, with his own glance around the room, he finds his voice again: "Damn those guards," he booms. "The perimeter's been breached."

* * * *

"Blanche DuBois," Pete says later, when it's just the two of them alone in the house, lying side by side in the darkness.

The body has been removed, and Beatrice and Dwight have been called. They'll drive in the next morning. They'll handle things now. The police took the Colonel away for questioning, for evaluation, and Keri began straightening up, picking up glass, rubbing at the paint on the cabinets, until Pete took her in his arms and held her tight and told her it was time for bed, time to let go, at least for the night.

But she couldn't do that, of course. For a while, staring at the ceiling, Keri has listened to the silence of the house, believed that she could hear the old man's absence somewhere in it. Pete has seemed far away in his own thoughts, reflecting on the loss in his own way, Keri thinks, until those sudden words of his.

"What?" she asks. She doesn't turn to look at him.

"Blanche DuBois," he says. "Tennessee Williams. *Streetcar Named Desire*. 'I've always relied on the kindness of strangers.'" Pete tries out a Southern drawl, not as good as his British voice, though it strikes her now that none of his accents is very good. "I'd thought of the Colonel like Lear, you know, but tonight, watching him with the police when they took him away, the way he stood up straight, the way he walked… Pure Blanche DuBois. Living in his own world, his delusions, the long gone past."

"He was brave," Keri says. There's light on the ceiling, from the moonlight shining down through the window and reflecting somehow off the bedspread. "Gallant."

"Gallant," Pete echoes. "But that's the tragedy of it, isn't it? The way that we take the Stella role—all of us, the reader, the audience—

trying to keep the illusions aloft, maybe even believing in them a little."

In the blankness of the ceiling, Keri imagines Pete in the front of the class, pacing and gesturing, holding forth, the tweed jacket, patches on the sleeve. There's pride in those patches and a strut in his step, and she's sure she heard a snicker when he repeated the word *gallant*, as if he was marking up her term paper and dissatisfied somehow with the logic of her argument.

"When you say tragedy," she asks, "are you talking about the Colonel or about Blanche?"

He shrugs beside her, a laying-down shrug, shoulders shuffling against the pillow.

"Either," he says. "Both. Killing your daughter, not knowing it. That has all the elements of something classical, doesn't it?"

Later, many years later, lying in another bed with another man, and with her children with that husband nestled safely in their own beds just down the hallway, Keri will think back once more on this night and wonder yet again if this was the exact moment when things ended between them or if it was just one in a progression of such moments that took too long to accumulate. She'll wonder again why she stayed so long with him after this night, why she didn't just get up then and walk out into the darkness, up that gravel drive—off base once and for all. Illusions, she'll think. And tragedy. And she'll think of the hundred things she might have told Pete, the hundred times she might have told him. Then she'll remind herself: *But maybe it was enough.*

"He said her name," she tells Pete. "The Colonel. After he turned on the lights and saw her there, before he wandered out into the yard, he said 'Claire' because he saw her, what she'd done, and what he'd done, too. But first, just before that… He was looking for *me*, I know he was. Looking *out* for me. Before he said her name, he said mine. He called out for me. For the first time, he said Keri."

Art Taylor's fiction has appeared in *Ellery Queen's Mystery Magazine* and *North American Review*; online at *Fiction Weekly, Prick of the Spindle*, and *SmokeLong Quarterly*; and in various regional publications. His story "A Voice from the Past" was short-listed for the 2010 *Best American Mystery Stories* anthology. He regularly reviews crime fiction for the *Washington Post* and contributes frequently to *Mystery Scene*. A native of Richlands, N.C., he graduated from Yale University and earned writing degrees from N.C. State and from George Mason University, where he is now an assistant professor of English. More information can be found at arttaylorwriter.com.

ABOUT THE EDITORS

Donna Andrews's biography can be found at the end of her story in this book.

Ellen Crosby is the author of a series of six mysteries set in Virginia wine country, including her most recent novel, *The Sauvignon Secret* (Scribner, 2011). She has also written *Moscow Nights*, a standalone novel published in the United Kingdom, and is currently at work on a new series featuring a Washington, D.C., photojournalist. Previously she worked as a freelance reporter for the *Washington Post*, a Moscow correspondent for ABC News Radio, and an economist at the U.S. Senate. Ellen lives in Virginia with her family. Visit her website at www.ellencrosby.com.

Barb Goffman's biography can be found at the end of her story in this book.

Sandra Parshall is the Agatha Award-winning author of the Rachel Goddard mysteries, which include *The Heat of the Moon*, *Disturbing the Dead*, *Broken Places*, and *Under the Dog Star*. She lives in Northern Virginia with her husband and cats and is a long-time member of the Chesapeake Chapter of Sisters in Crime and former member of the national Sisters in Crime board.

Daniel Stashower is a two-time Edgar-award winner whose most recent nonfiction books are *The Beautiful Cigar Girl* and (as coeditor) *Arthur Conan Doyle: A Life in Letters*. Dan is also the author of five mystery novels, and has received the Agatha and Anthony awards. His short stories have appeared in numerous anthologies, including *The Best American Mystery Stories* and *The World's Finest Mystery and Crime Stories*. He lives in Washington, D.C., with his wife and their two sons.

Marcia Talley is the Agatha and Anthony award-winning author of eleven mysteries featuring survivor and sleuth Hannah

Ives. Marcia's first mystery, *Sing It To Her Bones*, won the Malice Domestic grant and was nominated for an Agatha Award. Ten mysteries followed that early success, including three IMBA bestsellers. Hannah's eleventh adventure, *The Last Refuge*, was released in early 2012. Her short stories appear in more than a dozen collections. Marcia served as president of Sisters in Crime, and is a member of Mystery Writers of America, the Authors' Guild, and the Crime Writers Association. She divides her time between Annapolis, Maryland, and living aboard an antique sailboat in the Bahamas.

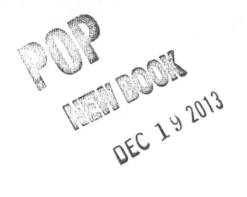

CPSIA information can be obtained at www.ICGtesting.com
Printed in the USA
LVOW05s2327011213

363457LV00001B/356/P

9 781434 440600